My Lady
Caprice

My Lady Caprice

By
Jeffery Farnol

With illustrations by
Charlotte Weber Ditzler
and decorations by
Theodore B. Hapgood

New York
Dodd, Mead & Company
1907

Contents

Illustrations

My Lady
Caprice

My Lady Caprice

I
TREASURE TROVE

I SAT fishing. I had not caught anything,
of course—I rarely do, nor am I fond
of fishing in the very smallest degree,
but I fished assiduously all the same,
because circumstances demanded it.

It had all come about through Lady
Warburton, Lisbeth's maternal aunt.
Who Lisbeth is you will learn if you
trouble to read these veracious narratives—suffice it for the present that
she has been an orphan from her
youth up, with no living relative save
her married sister Julia and her Aunt
(with a capital A)—the Lady Warburton aforesaid.

Lady Warburton is small and somewhat bony, with a sharp chin and a sharper nose, and invariably uses lorgnette; also, she is possessed of much worldly goods.

Precisely a week ago Lady Warburton had requested me to call upon her—had regarded me with a curious exactitude through her lorgnette, and gently though firmly (Lady Warburton is always firm) had suggested that Elizabeth, though a dear child, was young and inclined to be a little self-willed. That she (Lady Warburton) was of opinion that Elizabeth had mistaken the friendship which had existed between us so long for something stronger. That although she (Lady Warburton) quite appreciated the fact that one who wrote books, and occasionally a play, was not necessarily immoral—still I was, of course, a terrible Bohemian, and the air of Bohemia was not calculated to conduce to that degree of matrimonial harmony which she (Lady Warburton) as Elizabeth's Aunt, standing to her in place of a mother, could wish for. That, therefore, under these circumstances my attentions were—etc., etc.

Here I would say in justice to myself that despite the torrent of her eloquence I had at first made some attempt at resistance; but who could hope to contend successfully against a woman possessed of such an indomitable nose and chin, and one, moreover, who could level a pair of lorgnette with such deadly precision? Still, had Lisbeth been beside me things might have been different even then; but she had gone away into the country—so Lady Warburton had informed me. Thus alone and at her mercy, she had succeeded in wringing from me a half promise that I would cease my attentions for the space of six months, "just to give dear Eliza-

beth time to learn her own heart in regard to the matter."

This was last Monday. On the
Wednesday following, as I wandered
aimlessly along Piccadilly, at odds
with Fortune and myself, but especially with myself, my eye encountered
the Duchess of Chelsea.

The Duchess is familiarly known as
the "Conversational Brook" from the
fact that when once she begins she
goes on forever. Hence, being in my
then frame of mind, it was with a
feeling of rebellion that I obeyed the
summons of her parasol and crossed
over to the brougham.

"So she's gone away?" was her
greeting as I raised my hat—"Lisbeth," she nodded, "I happened to
hear something about her, you know."

It is strange, perhaps, but the Duchess generally does "happen to hear"
something about everything.

"And you actually allowed yourself

to be bullied into making that promise—Dick! Dick! I'm ashamed of you."

"How was I to help myself?" I began. "You see——"

"Poor boy!" said the Duchess, patting me affectionately with the handle of her parasol, "it wasn't to be expected. of course. You see, I know her—many, many years ago I was at school with Agatha Warburton."

"But she probably didn't use lorgnettes then, and——"

"Her nose was just as sharp though—'peaky' I used to call it," nodded the Duchess. "And she has actually sent Lisbeth away—dear child—and to such a horrid, quiet little place, too, where she'll have nobody to talk to but that young Selwyn——"

"I beg pardon, Duchess, but——"

"Horace Selwyn, of Selwyn Park—cousin to Lord Selwyn, of Brankesmere. Agatha has been scheming for it a long time, under the rose, you know. Of course, it would be a good match, in a way—wealthy, and all that—but I must say he bores me horribly—so very serious and precise!"

"Really!" I exclaimed, "do you mean to say——"

"I expect she will have them married before they know it—Agatha's dreadfully determined. Her character lies in her nose and chin."

"But Lisbeth is not a child—she has a will of her own, and——"

"True," nodded the Duchess, "but is it a match for Agatha's chin? And then, too, it is rather more than possible that you are become the object of her bitterest scorn by now."

"But, my dear Duchess——"

"Oh, Agatha is a born diplomat. Of course she has written before this, and without actually saying it has managed to convey the fact that you are a monster of perfidy; and Lisbeth, poor child, is probably crying her eyes out, or imagining she hates you, is ready to accept the first proposal she receives out of pure pique."

"Great heavens!" I exclaimed, "what on earth can I do?"

"You might go fishing," the Duchess suggested thoughtfully.

"Fishing!" I repeated, "—er, to be sure, but——"

"Riverdale is a very pretty place they tell me," pursued the Duchess in the same thoughtful tone; "there is a house there, a fine old place called Fane Court. It stands facing the river, and adjoins Selwyn Park, I believe."

"Duchess," I exclaimed, as I jotted down the address upon my cuff, "I owe you a debt of gratitude that I can never——"

"Tut, tut!" said her Grace.

"I think I'll start to-day, and——"

"You really couldn't do better," nodded the Duchess.

*   *   *   *   *

And so it befell that upon this August afternoon I sat in the shade of the alders fishing, with the smoke of my pipe floating up into the sunshine. By adroit questioning I had elicited from mine host of the Three Jolly Anglers the precise whereabouts of Fane Court, the abode of Lisbeth's sister, and guided by his directions, had chosen this sequestered spot, where by simply turning my head I could catch a glimpse of its tall chimneys above the swaying green of treetops.

It is a fair thing upon a hot summer's afternoon within some shady bower to lie upon one's back and stare up through a network of branches into the limitless blue beyond, while the air is full of the stir of leaves, and the murmur of water among the reeds. Or propped on lazy elbow, to watch perspiring wretches, short of breath and purple of visage, urge boats up stream or down, each deluding himself into the belief that he is enjoying it. Life under such conditions may seem very fair, as I say; yet I was not happy. The words of the Duchess seemed everywhere about me.

"You are become the object of her bitterest scorn by now," sobbed the wind.

"You are become," etc., etc., moaned the river. It was therefore with no little trepidation that I looked forward to my meeting with Lisbeth.

It was at this moment that the bushes parted and a boy appeared. He was a somewhat diminutive boy, clad in a velvet suit with a lace collar, both of which were plentifully bespattered with mud. He carried his shoes and stockings beneath one arm, and in the other hand swung a hazel branch. He stood with his little brown legs well apart, regarding me with a critical eye; but when at length he spoke his attitude was decidedly friendly.

"Hallo, man!"

"Hallo," I returned; "and whom may you be?"

"Well," he answered gravely, "my real name is Reginald Augustus, but they call me 'The Imp.'"

"I can well believe it," I said, eyeing his muddy person.

"If you please, what is an imp?"

"An imp," I explained, "is a sort of an—angel."

"But," he demurred, after a moment's thought, "I haven't got any wings an' things—or a trumpet."

"Your kind never do have wings, or trumpets."

"Oh, I see," he said; and sitting down began to wipe the mud from his legs with his stockings.

"Rather muddy, aren't you?" I

hinted. The boy cast a furtive glance at his draggled person.

" 'Fraid I'm a teeny bit wet, too," he said hesitatingly. "You see, I've been playing at 'Romans,' an' I had to wade, you know, 'cause I was the standard-bearer who jumped into the sea waving his sword an' crying, 'Follow me!' You remember him, don't you?—he's in the history book."

"To be sure," I nodded; "a truly heroic character. But if you were the Romans, where were the ancient Britons?"

"Oh, they were the reeds, you know; you ought to have seen me slay them. It was fine; they went down like—like——"

"Corn before the sickle," I suggested.

"Yes, just!" he cried; "the battle raged for hours."

"You must be rather tired."

" 'Course not," he answered, with an indignant look. "I'm not a girl—an' I'm nearly nine, too."

"I gather from your tone that you are not partial to the sex—you don't like girls, eh, Imp?"

"Should think not," he returned; "silly things, girls are. There's Dorothy, you know; we were playing at executions the other day—she was Mary Queen of Scots an' I was the headsman. I made a lovely axe with wood and silver paper, you know; an' when I cut her head off she cried awfully, an' I only gave her the weeniest little tap—an' they sent me to bed at six o'clock for it. I believe she cried on purpose—awfully caddish, wasn't it?"

"My dear Imp," said I, "the older you grow, the more the depravity of the sex will become apparent to you."

"Do you know, I like you," he said, regarding me thoughtfully. "I think you are fine."

"Now that's very nice of you, Imp; in common with my kind I have a weakness for flattery—please go on."

"I mean, I think you are jolly."

"As to that," I said, shaking my head and sighing, "appearances are often very deceptive; at the heart of many a fair blossom there is a canker worm."

"I'm awfull' fond of worms, too," said the Imp.

"Indeed?"

"Yes. I got a pocketful yesterday, only Aunty found out an' made me let them all go again."

"Ah—yes," I said sympathetically; "that was the woman of it."

"I've only got one left now," continued the Imp; and thrusting a hand into the pocket of his knickerbockers he drew forth six inches or so of slimy worm and held it out to me upon his small, grimy palm.

"He's nice and fat!" I said.

"Yes," nodded the Imp; "I caught him under the gooseberry bushes;" and dropping it back into his pocket he proceeded to don his shoes and stockings.

" 'Fraid I'm a bit muddy," he said suddenly.

"Oh, you might be worse," I answered reassuringly.

"Do you think they'll notice it?" he inquired, contorting himself horribly in order to view the small of his back.

"Well," I hesitated, "it all depends, you know."

"I don't mind Dorothy, or Betty the cook, or the governess—it's Auntie Lisbeth I'm thinking about."

"Auntie—who?" I exclaimed, regardless of grammar.

"Auntie Lisbeth," repeated the Imp.

"What is she like?"

"Oh, she's grown up big, only she's nice. She came to take care of Dorothy an' me while mother goes away to get nice an' strong—oh, Auntie Lisbeth's jolly, you know."

"With black hair and blue eyes?" The Imp nodded.

"And a dimple at the corner of her mouth?" I went on dreamily—"a dimple that would lead a man to the—Old Gentleman himself?"

"What old gentleman?"

"Oh, a rather disreputable old gentleman," I answered evasively.

"An' do you know my Auntie Lisbeth?"

"I think it extremely probable—in fact, I'm sure of it."

"Then you might lend me your handkerchief, please; I tied mine to a bush for a flag, you know, an' it blew away."

"You'd better come here and I'll give you a rub-down, my Imp." He obeyed, with many profuse expressions of gratitude.

"Have you got any Aunties?" he inquired, as I laboured upon his miry person.

"No," I answered, shaking my head; "unfortunately mine are all Aunts, and that is vastly different."

"Oh," said the Imp, regarding me with a puzzled expression; "are they nice—I mean do they ever read to you out of the history book, an' help you to sail boats, an' paddle?"

"Paddle?" I repeated.

"Yes. My Auntie Lisbeth does. The other day we got up awfull' early an' went for a walk, an' we came to the river, so we took off our shoes an' stockings an' we paddled; it was ever so jolly, you know. An' when Auntie wasn't looking I found a frog an' put it in her stocking."

"Highly strategic, my Imp! Well?"

"It was awful funny," he said, smiling dreamily. "When she went to put it on she gave a little high-up scream, like Dorothy does when I pinch her a

bit—an' then she throwed them both
away, 'cause she was afraid there was
frogs in both of them. Then she put
on her shoes without any stockings at
all, so I hid them."

"Where?" I cried eagerly.

"Reggie!" called a voice some distance away—a voice I recognised with
a thrill. "Reggie!"

"Imp, would you like half a crown?"

"'Course I would; but you might
clean my back, please," and he began
rubbing himself feverishly with his
cap, after the fashion of a scrubbing
brush.

"Look here," I said, pulling out the
coin, "tell me where you hid them—
quick—and I'll give you this." The
Imp held out his hand, but even as he
did so the bushes parted and Lisbeth
stood before us. She gave a little, low
cry of surprise at sight of me, and then
frowned.

"You?" she exclaimed.

"Yes," I answered, raising my cap. And there I stopped, trying frantically to remember the speech I had so carefully prepared—the greeting which was to have explained my conduct and disarmed her resentment at the very outset. But rack my brain as I would, I could think of nothing but the reproach in her eyes—her disdainful mouth and chin—and that one haunting phrase:

" 'I suppose I am become the object of your bitterest scorn by now?' " I found myself saying.

"My aunt informed me of—of everything, and naturally——"

"Let me explain," I began.

"Really, it is not at all necessary."

"But, Lisbeth, I must—I insist——"

"Reginald," she said, turning toward the Imp, who was still busy with his cap, "it's nearly tea-time, and—why, whatever have you been doing to yourself?"

"For the last half hour," I interposed, "we have been exchanging our opinions on the sex."

"An' talking 'bout worms," added the Imp. "This man is fond of worms, too, Auntie Lisbeth—I like him."

"Thanks," I said; "but let me beg of you to drop your very distant mode of address. Call me Uncle Dick."

"But you're not my Uncle Dick, you know," he demurred.

"Not yet, perhaps; but there's no knowing what may happen some day if your Auntie thinks us worthy—so take time by the forelock, my Imp, and call me Uncle Dick."

Whatever Lisbeth might or might not have said was checked by the patter of footsteps, and a little girl tripped into view, with a small, fluffy kitten cuddled in her arms.

"Oh, Auntie Lisbeth," she began, but stopped to stare at me over the back of the fluffy kitten.

"Hallo, Dorothy!" cried the Imp; "this is Uncle Dick. You can come an' shake hands with him if you like."

"I didn't know I had an Uncle Dick," said Dorothy, hesitating.

"Oh, yes; it's all right," answered the Imp reassuringly. "I found him, you know, an' he likes worms, too!" Dorothy gave me her hand demurely.

"How do you do, Uncle Dick?" she said in a quaint, old-fashioned way. "Reginald is always finding things, you know, an' he likes worms, too!" Dorothy gave me her hand demurely.

From somewhere near by there came the silvery chime of a bell.

"Why, there's the tea-bell!" exclaimed Lisbeth; "and, Reginald, you have to change those muddy clothes. Say good-bye to Mr. Brent, children, and come along."

"Imp," I whispered as the others

" ' But you're not my Uncle Dick,
you know ' "

turned away, "where did you hide those stockings?" And I slipped the half crown into his ready palm.

"Along the river there's a tree—very big an' awfull' fat, you know, with a lot of stickie-out branches, an' a hole in its stomach—they're in there."

"Reginald!" called Lisbeth.

"Up stream or down?"

"That way," he answered, pointing vaguely down stream; and with a nod that brought the yellow curls over his eyes he scampered off.

"Along the river," I repeated, "in a big, fat tree with a lot of stickie-out branches!" It sounded a trifle indefinite, I thought—still I could but try. So having packed up my rod I set out upon the search.

It was strange, perhaps, but nearly every tree I saw seemed to be either "big" or "fat"—and all of them had "stickie-out" branches.

Thus the sun was already low in the

west, and I was lighting my fifth pipe when I at length observed the tree in question.

A great pollard oak it was, standing upon the very edge of the stream, easily distinguishable by its unusual size and the fact that at some time or another it had been riven by lightning. After all, the Imp's description had been in the main correct; it was "fat," immensely fat; and I hurried joyfully forward.

I was still some way off when I saw the distant flutter of a white skirt, and—yes, sure enough, there was Lisbeth, walking quickly, too, and she was a great deal nearer the tree than I.

Prompted by a sudden conviction, I dropped my rod and began to run. Immediately Lisbeth began running, too. I threw away my creel and sprinted **for** all I was worth. I had earned some small fame at this sort of thing in my university days, yet I arrived at the tree with only a very few yards to spare. Throwing myself upon my knees, I commenced a feverish search, and presently—more by good fortune than anything else—my random fingers encountered a soft, silken bundle. When Lisbeth came up, flushed and panting, I held them in my hands.

"Give them to me!" she cried.

"I'm sorry——"

"Please," she begged.

"I'm very sorry——"

"Mr. Brent," said Lisbeth, drawing herself up, "I'll trouble you for my—them."

"Pardon me, Lisbeth," I answered, "but if I remember anything of the law of 'treasure-trove' one of these should go to the Crown, and one belongs to me."

Lisbeth grew quite angry—one of her few bad traits.

"You will give them up at once—
immediately."

"On the contrary," I said very gently, "seeing the Crown can have no
use for one, I shall keep them both to
dream over when the nights are long
and lonely."

Lisbeth actually stamped her foot at
me, and I tucked "them" into my
pocket.

"How did you know they—they
were here?" she inquired after a pause.

"I was directed to a tree with 'stickie-
out' branches," I answered.

"Oh, that Imp!" she exclaimed, and
stamped her foot again.

"Do you know, I've grown quite at-
tached to that nephew of mine already?" I said.

"He's not a nephew of yours," cried
Lisbeth quite hotly.

"Not legally, perhaps; that is where
you might be of such assistance to us
Lisbeth. A boy with only an aunt

here and there is unbalanced, so to
speak; he requires the stronger influence of an uncle. Not," I continued
hastily, "that I would depreciate
aunts—by the way, he has but
one, I believe?" Lisbeth nodded
coldly.

"Of course," I nodded; "and very
lucky in that one—extremely fortu-
nate. Now, years ago, when I was
a boy, I had three, and all of them
blanks, so to speak. I mean none of
them ever read to me out of the history book, or helped me to sail boats,
or paddled and lost their— No,
mine used to lecture me about my hair
and nails, I remember, and glare at
me over the big tea urn until I choked
into my teacup. A truly desolate
childhood mine. I had no big-fisted
uncle to thump me persuasively when
I needed it; had fortune granted me
one I might have been a very different
man, Lisbeth. You behold in me a

horrible example of what one may become whose boyhood has been denuded of uncles."

"If you will be so very obliging as to return my—my property."

"My dear Lisbeth," I sighed, "be reasonable; suppose we talk of something else;" and I attempted, though quite vainly, to direct her attention to the glories of the sunset.

A fallen tree lay near by, upon which Lisbeth seated herself with a certain determined set of her little, round chin that I knew well.

"And how long do you intend keeping me here?" she asked in a resigned tone.

"Always, if I had my way."

"Really?" she said, and whole volumes could never describe all the scorn she managed to put into that single word. "You see," she continued, "after what Aunt Agatha wrote and told me——"

"Lisbeth," I broke in, "if you'll only——"

"I naturally supposed——"

"If you'll only let me explain——"

"That you would abide by the promise you made her and wait——"

"Until you knew your own heart," I put in. "The question is, how long will it take you? Probably, if you would allow me to teach you——"

"Your presence here now stamps you as—as horribly deceitful!"

"Undoubtedly," I nodded; "but you see when I was foolish enough to give that promise your very excellent Aunt made no reference to her intentions regarding a certain Mr. Selwyn."

"Oh!" exclaimed Lisbeth. And feeling that I had made a point, I continued with redoubled ardour:

"She gave me to understand that she merely wished you to have time to know your own heart in the matter. Now, as I said before, how long will it take you to find out, Lisbeth?"

She sat chin in hand staring straight before her, and her black brows were still drawn together in a frown. But I watched her mouth—just where the scarlet underlip curved up to meet its fellow.

Lisbeth's mouth is a trifle wide, perhaps, and rather full-lipped, and somewhere at one corner—I can never be quite certain of its exact location, because its appearance is, as a rule, so very meteoric—but somewhere there is a dimple. Now, if ever there was an arrant traitor in this world it is that dimple; for let her expression be ever so guileless, let her wistful eyes be raised with a look of tears in their blue depths, despite herself that dimple will spring into life and undo it all in a moment. So it was now, even as I watched it quivered round her lips, and feeling herself betrayed, the frown vanished altogether and she smiled.

"And now, Dick, suppose you give me my—my——"

"Conditionally," I said, sitting down beside her.

The sun had set, and from somewhere among the purple shadows of the wood the rich, deep notes of a blackbird came to us, with pauses now and then, filled in with the rustle of leaves and the distant lowing of cows.

"Not far from the village of Down in Kent," I began dreamily, "there stands an old house with quaint, high-gabled roofs and twisted Tudor chimneys. Many years ago it was the home of fair ladies and gallant gentlemen, but its glory is long past. And yet, Lisbeth, when I think of it at such an hour as this, and with you beside me, I begin to wonder if we could not manage between us to bring back the old order of things."

Lisbeth was silent.

"It has a wonderful old-fashioned rose garden, and you are fond of roses, Lisbeth."

"Yes," she murmured; "I'm very fond of roses."

"They would be in full bloom now," I suggested.

There was another pause, during which the blackbird performed three or four difficult arias with astonishing ease and precision.

"Aunt Agatha is fond of roses, too!" said Lisbeth at last very gravely. "Poor, dear Aunt, I wonder what she would say if she could see us now?"

"Such things are better left to the imagination," I answered.

"I ought to write and tell her," murmured Lisbeth.

"But you won't do that, of course?"

"No, I won't do that, if——"

"Well?"

"If you will give me—them."

"One," I demurred.

"Both!"

"On one condition, then—just once, Lisbeth?"

Her lips were very near, her lashes drooped, and for one delicious moment she hesitated. Then I felt a little tug at my coat pocket, and springing to her feet she was away with "them" clutched in her hand.

"Trickery!" I cried, and started in pursuit.

There is a path through the woods leading to the Shrubbery at Fane Court. Down this she fled, and her laughter came to me on the wind. I was close upon her when she reached the gate, and darting through, turned, flushed but triumphant.

"I've won!" she mocked, nodding her head at me.

"Who can cope with the duplicity of a woman?" I retorted. "But, Lisbeth, you will give me one—just one?"

"It would spoil the pair."

"Oh, very well," I sighed, "good-night, Lisbeth," and lifting my cap I turned away.

There came a ripple of laughter behind me, something struck me softly upon the cheek, and stooping, I picked up that which lay half unrolled at my feet, but when I looked round Lisbeth was gone.

"So presently I thrust "them" into my pocket and walked back slowly along the river path toward the hospitable shelter of the Three Jolly Anglers.

II

THE SHERIFF OF NOTTINGHAM

To sit beside a river on a golden afternoon listening to its whispered melody, while the air about one is fragrant with summer, and heavy with
the drone of unseen wings!—What
ordinary mortal could wish for more?

And yet, though conscious of this
fair world about me, I was still un-
content, for my world was incomplete
—nay, lacked its most essential charm,
and I sat with my ears on the stretch,
waiting for Lisbeth's chance footstep
on the path and the soft whisper of
her skirts.

The French are indeed a great people, for among many other things they
alone have caught that magic sound
a woman's garments make as she

walks, and given it to the world in the one word *"frou-frou."*

O wondrous word! O word sublime! How full art thou of delicate suggestion! Truly, there can be no sweeter sound to ears masculine upon a golden summer afternoon—or any other time, for that matter—than the soft *"frou-frou"* that tells him *She* is coming.

At this point my thoughts were interrupted by something which hurtled through the air and splashed into the water at my feet. Glancing at this object, I recognised the loud-toned cricket cap affected by the Imp, and reaching for it, I fished it out on the end of my rod. It was a hideous thing of red, white, blue, and green—a really horrible affair, and therefore much prized by its owner, as I knew.

Behind me the bank rose some four or five feet, crowned with willows and underbrush, from the other side of

which there now came a prodigious
rustling and panting. Rising to my
feet, therefore, I parted the leaves
with extreme care, and beheld the Imp
himself.

He was armed to the teeth—that is
to say, a wooden sword swung at his
thigh, a tin bugle depended from his
belt, and he carried a bow and arrow.
Opposite him was another boy, particularly ragged at knee and elbow, who
stood with hands thrust into his pockets and grinned.

"Base caitiff, hold!" cried the Imp,
fitting an arrow to the string; "stand
an' deliver. Give me my cap, thou
varlet, thou!" The boy's grin ex-
panded.

"Give me my cap, base slave, or I'll
shoot you—by my troth!" As he
spoke the Imp aimed his arrow,
whereupon the boy ducked promptly.

"I ain't got yer cap," he grinned
from the shelter of his arm. "It's

been an' gone an' throwed itself into
the river!" The Imp let fly his arrow, which was answered by a yell
from the Base Varlet.

"Yah!" he cried derisively as the Imp
drew his sword with a melodramatic
flourish. "Yah! put down that stick
an' I'll fight yer."

The Imp indignantly repudiated his
trusty weapon being called "a stick"—
"an' I don't think," he went on, "that
Robin Hood ever fought without his
sword. Let's see what the book says,"
and he drew a very crumpled paper-
covered volume from his pocket, which
he consulted with knitted brows, while
the Base Varlet watched him, open-
mouthed.

"Oh, yes," nodded the Imp; "it's all
right. Listen to this!" and he read as
follows in a stern, deep voice:

" 'Then Robin tossed aside his trusty
blade, an' laying bare his knotted arm,
approached the dastardly ruffian with

many a merry quip and jest, prepared
for the fierce death-grip.' "

Hereupon the Imp laid aside his
book and weapons and proceeded to
roll up his sleeve, having done which
to his satisfaction, he faced round
upon the Base Varlet.

"Have at ye, dastardly ruffian!" he
cried, and therewith ensued a battle,
fierce and fell.

If his antagonist had it in height, the
Imp made up for it in weight—he is
a particularly solid Imp—and thus
the struggle lasted for some five minutes without any appreciable advan-
tage to either, when, in eluding one of
the enemy's desperate rushes, the Imp
stumbled, lost his balance, and next
moment I had caught him in my arms.
For a space "the enemy" remained
panting on the bank above, and then
with another yell turned and darted
off among the bushes.

"Hallo, Imp!" I said.

"Hallo, Uncle Dick!" he returned.

"Hurt?" I inquired.

"Wounded a bit in the nose, you know," he answered, mopping that organ with his handkerchief; "but did you see me punch 'yon varlet' in the eye?"

"Did you, Imp?"

"I think so, Uncle Dick; only I do wish I'd made him surrender. The book says that Robin Hood always made his enemies 'surrender an' beg their life on trembling knee!' Oh, it must be fine to see your enemies on their knee!"

"Especially if they tremble," I added.

"Do you s'pose that boy—I mean 'yon base varlet' would have surrendered?"

"Not a doubt of it—if he hadn't happened to push you over the bank first."

"Oh!" murmured the Imp rather dubiously.

MY LADY CAPRICE

"By the way," I said as I filled my pipe, "where is your Auntie Lisbeth?"

"Well, I chased her up the big apple-tree with my bow an' arrow."

"Of course," I nodded. "Very right and proper!"

"You see," he explained, "I wanted her to be a wild elephant an' she wouldn't."

"Extremely disobliging of her!"

"Yes, wasn't it? So when she was right up I took away the ladder an' hid it."

"Highly strategic, my Imp."

"So then I turned into Robin Hood. I hung my cap on a bush to shoot at, you know, an' 'the Base Varlet' came up an' ran off with it."

"And there it is," I said, pointing to where it lay. The Imp received it with profuse thanks, and having wrung out the water, clapped it upon his curls and sat down beside me.

"I found another man who wants to be my uncle," he began.

"Oh, indeed?"

"Yes; but I don't want any more, you know."

"Of course not. One like me suffices for your every-day needs—eh, my Imp?"

The Imp nodded. "It was yesterday," he continued. "He came to see Auntie Lisbeth, an' I found them in the summer-house in the orchard. An' I heard him say, 'Miss Elizabeth, you're prettier than ever!'"

"Did he though, confound him!"

"Yes, an' then Auntie Lisbeth looked silly, an' then he saw me behind a tree an' he looked silly, too. Then he said, 'Come here, little man!' An' I went, you know, though I do hate to be called 'little man.' Then he said he'd give me a shilling if I'd call him Uncle Frank."

"And what did you answer?"

" 'Fraid I'm awfull' wicked," sighed the Imp, shaking his head, " 'cause I told him a great big lie."

"Did you, Imp?"

"Yes. I said I didn't want his shilling, an' I do, you know, most awfully, to buy a spring pistol with."

"Oh, well, we'll see what can be done about the spring pistol," I answered. "And so you don't like him, eh?"

"Should think not," returned the Imp promptly. "He's always so—so awfull' clean, an' wears a little moustache with teeny sharp points on it."

"Any one who does that deserves all he gets," I said, shaking my head. And what is his name?"

"The Honourable Frank Selwyn, an' he lives at Selwyn Park—the next house to ours."

"Oho!" I exclaimed, and whistled.

"Uncle Dick" said the Imp, breaking in upon a somewhat unpleasant train of thought conjured up by this intelli-

gence, "will you come an' be 'Little-
John under the merry greenwood
tree'? Do."

"Why, what do you know about 'the
merry greenwood,' Imp?"

"Oh, lots!" he answered, hastily
pulling out the tattered book. "This
is all about Robin Hood an' Little-
John. Ben, the gardener's boy, lent
it to me. Robin Hood was a fine
chap, an' so was Little-John, an' they
used to set ambushes an' capture the
Sheriff of Nottingham an' all sorts of
caddish barons, an' tie them to
trees."

"My Imp," I said, shaking my head,
"the times are sadly changed. One
cannot tie barons—caddish or otherwise—to trees in these degenerate
days."

"No, I s'pose not," sighed the Imp
dolefully; "but I do wish you would
be Little-John, Uncle Dick."

"Oh, certainly, Imp, if it will make

you any happier; though of a truth, bold Robin," I continued after the manner of the story books, "Little-John hath a mind to bide awhile and commune with himself here; yet give but one blast upon thy bugle horn and thou shalt find my arm and quarter-staff ready and willing enough, I'll warrant you!"

"That sounds awfull' fine, Uncle Dick, only—you haven't got a quar-ter-staff, you know."

"Yea, 'tis here!" I answered, and detached the lower joint of my fishing rod. The Imp rose, and folding his arms, surveyed me as Robin Hood himself might have done—that is to say, with an 'eye of fire.'

"So be it, my faithful Little-John," quoth he; "meet me at the Blasted Oak at midnight. An' if I shout for help—I mean blow my bugle—you'll come an' rescue me, won't you, Uncle Dick?"

"Ay; trust me for that," I answered, all unsuspecting.

" 'Tis well!" nodded the Imp; and with a wave of his hand he turned and scrambling up the bank disappeared.

Of the existence of Mr. Selwyn I was already aware, having been notified in this particular by the Duchess, as I have told in the foregoing narrative.

Now, a rival in air—in the abstract, so to speak—is one thing, but a rival who was on a sufficiently intimate footing to deal in personal compliments, and above all, one who was already approved of and encouraged by the powers that be, in the person of Lady Warburton — Lisbeth's formidable aunt—was another consideration altogether.

"Miss Elizabeth, you're prettier than ever!"

Somehow the expression rankled.

What right had he to tell her such things?—and in a summer-house, too;

—the insufferable audacity of the fellow!

A pipe being indispensable to the occasion, I took out my matchbox, only to find that it contained but a solitary vesta.

The afternoon had been hot and still hitherto, with never so much as a breath of wind stirring; but no sooner did I prepare to strike that match than from somewhere — Heaven knows where—there came a sudden flaw of wind that ruffled the glassy waters of the river and set every leaf whispering. Waiting until what I took to be a favourable opportunity, with infinite precaution I struck a light. It flickered in a sickly fashion for a moment between my sheltering palms, and immediately expired.

This is but one example of that "Spirit of the Perverse" pervading all things mundane, which we poor mortals are called upon to bear as best we

may. Therefore I tossed aside the
charred match, and having searched
fruitlessly through my pockets for another, waited philosophically for some
"good Samaritan" to come along.
The bank I have mentioned sloped
away gently on my left, thus afford-
ing an uninterrupted view of the
path.

Now as my eyes followed this winding path I beheld an individual some
distance away who crawled upon his
hands and knees, evidently searching
for something. As I watched, he succeeded in raking a Panama hat from
beneath a bush, and having dusted it
carefully with his handkerchief, re-
placed it upon his head and continued
his advance.

With some faint hope that there
might be a loose match hiding away
in some corner of my pockets, I went
through them again more carefully,
but alas! with no better success;

whereupon I gave it up and turned to glance at the approaching figure.

My astonishment may be readily imagined when I beheld him in precisely the same attitude as before—that is to say, upon his hands and knees.

I was yet puzzling over this phenomenon when he again raked out the Panama on the end of the hunting-crop he carried, dusted it as before, looking about him the while with a bewildered air, and setting it firmly upon his head, came down the path.

He was a tall young fellow, scrupulously neat and well groomed from the polish of his brown riding boots to his small, sleek moustache, which was parted with elaborate care and twisted into two fine points. There was about his whole person an indefinable air of self-complacent satisfaction, but he carried his personality in his moustache, so to speak, which, though small, as I say, and precise to a hair, yet obtruded itself upon one in a vaguely unpleasant way. Noticing all this, I thought I might make a very good guess as to his identity if need were.

All at once, as I watched him—like a bird rising from her nest—the devoted Panama rose in the air, turned over once or twice and fluttered (I use the word figuratively) into a bramble bush. Bad language was writ large in every line of his body as he stood looking about him, the hunting-crop quivering in his grasp.

It was at this precise juncture that his eye encountered me, and pausing only to recover his unfortunate headgear, he strode toward where I sat.

"Do you know anything about this?" he inquired in a somewhat aggressive manner, holding up a length of black thread.

"A piece of ordinary pack-thread,"

I answered, affecting to examine it with a critical eye.

"Do you know anything about it?" he said again, evidently in a very bad temper.

"Sir," I answered, "I do not."

"Because if I thought you did——"

"Sir," I broke in, "you'll excuse me, but that seems a very remarkable hat of yours."

"I repeat if I thought you did——"

"Of course," I went on, "each to his taste, but personally I prefer one with less 'gymnastic' and more 'stay-at-home, qualities."

The hunting-crop was raised threateningly.

"Mr. Selwyn?" I inquired in a conversational tone.

The hunting-crop hesitated and was lowered.

"Well, sir?"

"Ah, I thought so," I said, bowing; "permit me to trespass upon your generosity to the extent of a match—or, say, a couple."

Mr. Selwyn remained staring down at me for a moment, and I saw the points of his moustache positively curling with indignation. Then, without deigning a reply, he turned on his heel and strode away. He had not gone more than thirty or forty paces, however, when I heard him stop and swear savagely—I did not need to look to learn the reason—I admit I chuckled. But my merriment was short-lived, for a moment later came the feeble squeak of a horn followed by a shout and the Imp's voice upraised in dire distress.

"Little-John! Little-John! to the rescue!" it called.

I hesitated, for I will freely confess that when I had made that promise to the Imp it was with small expectation that I should be called upon to fulfil it. Still, a promise is a promise: so I sighed, and picking up the joint of my fishing rod, clambered up the bank. Glancing in the direction of the cries, I beheld Robin Hood struggling in the foe's indignant grasp.

Now, there were but two methods of procedure open to me as I could see— the serious or the frankly grotesque. Naturally I chose the latter, and quarter-staff on shoulder, I swaggered down the path with an air that Little-John himself might well have envied.

"Beshrew me!" I cried, confronting the amazed Mr. Selwyn, "who dares lay hands on bold Robin Hood?— away, base rogue, hie thee hence or I am like to fetch thee a dour ding on that pate o' thine!"

Mr. Selwyn loosed the Imp and stared at me in speechless astonishment, as well he might.

"Look ye, master," I continued, entering into the spirit of the thing, "no man lays hand on Robin Hood whiles

Little-John can twirl a staff or draw a bow-string—no, by St. Cuthbert!"

The Imp, retired to a safe distance, stood hearkening in a transport till, bethinking him of his part, he fished out the tattered book and began surreptitiously turning over the pages; as for Mr. Selwyn, he only fumbled at his moustache and stared.

"Aye, but I know thee," I went on again, "by thy sly and crafty look, by thy scallopped cape and chain of office, I know thee for that same Sheriff of Nottingham that hath sworn to our undoing. Go to! didst' think to take Robin—in the greenwood? Out upon thee! Thy years should have taught thee better wisdom. Out upon thee!"

"Now will I feed"—began the Imp, with the book carefully held behind him, "now will I feed fat mine vengeance—to thy knees for a scurvy rascal!"

"Aye, by St. Benedict!" I nodded,

MY LADY CAPRICE

" 'twere well he should do penance on his marrow-bones from hither to Nottingham Town; but as thou art strong —be merciful, Robin."

Mr. Selwyn still curled the point of his moustache.

"Are you mad," he inquired, "or only drunk?"

"As to that, good master Sheriff, it doth concern thee nothing—but mark you! 'tis an ill thing to venture within the greenwood whiles Robin Hood and Little-John be abroad."

Mr. Selwyn shrugged his shoulders and turned to the Imp.

"I am on my way to see your Aunt Elizabeth, and shall make it my particular care to inform her of your conduct, and to see that you are properly punished. As for you, sir," he continued, addressing me, "I shall inform the police that there is a madman at large."

At this double-barrelled threat the

Imp was plainly much dismayed, and coming up beside me, slipped his hand into mine, and I promptly pocketed it.

"Sweet master Sheriff," I said, sweeping off my cap in true outlaw fashion, "the way is long and something lonely; methinks—we will therefore e'en accompany you, and may perchance lighten the tedium with quip and quirk and a merry stave or so."

Seeing the angry rejoinder upon Mr. Selwyn's lips, I burst forth incontinent into the following ditty, the words extemporised to the tune of "Bonnie Dundee":

There lived a sheriff in Nottingham-
    shire,
  With a hey derry down and a
    down;
He was fond of good beef, but was
    fonder of beer,
  With a hey derry down and a down.

By the time we reached the Shrubbery gate the Imp was in an ecstasy and Mr. Selwyn once more reduced to speechless indignation and astonishment. Here our ways diverged, Mr. Selwyn turning toward the house, while the Imp and I made our way to the orchard at the rear.

"Uncle Dick," he said, halting suddenly, "do you think he will tell—really?"

"My dear Imp," I answered, "a man who wears 'points on his moustache' is capable of anything."

"Then I shall be sent to bed for it, I know I shall!"

"To run into a thread tied across the path must have been very annoying," I said, shaking my head thoughtfully, "especially with a brand-new hat!"

"They were only 'ambushes,' you know, Uncle Dick."

"To be sure," I nodded. "Now, observe, my Imp, here is a shilling; go and buy that spring-pistol you were speaking of, and take your time about it; I'll see what can be done in the meanwhile."

The Imp was reduced to incoherent thanks.

"That's all right," I said, "but you'd better hurry off."

He obeyed with alacrity, disappearing in the direction of the village, while I went on toward the orchard to find Lisbeth. And presently, sure enough, I did find her—that is to say, part of her, for the foliage of that particular tree happened to be very thick and I could see nothing of her but a foot.

A positively delicious foot it was, too, small and shapely, that swung audaciously to and fro; a foot in a ridiculously out-of-place little patent-leather shoe, with a sheen of slender silken ankle above.

I approached softly, with the soul of me in my eyes, so to speak, yet, despite my caution, she seemed to become aware of my presence in some way— the foot faltered in its swing and vanished as the leaves were parted and Lisbeth looked down at me.

"Oh, it's you?" she said, and I fancied she seemed quite pleased. "You'll find a step-ladder somewhere about— it can't be very far."

"Thanks," I answered, "but I don't want one."

"No; but *I* do; I want to get down. That little wretched Imp hid the ladder, and I've been here all the afternoon," she wailed.

"But then you refused to be an elephant, you know," I reminded her.

"He shall go to bed for it—directly after tea!" she said.

"Lisbeth," I returned, "I firmly believe your nature to be altogether too sweet and forgiving——"

"I want to come down!"

"Certainly," I said; "put your left foot in my right hand, take firm hold of the branch above and let yourself sink gently into my arms."

"Oh!" she exclaimed suddenly, "here's Mr. Selwyn coming," and following her glance, I saw a distant Panama approaching.

"Lisbeth," said I, "are you anxious to see him?"

"In this ridiculous situation—of course not!"

"Very well then, hide—just sit there and leave matters to me and——"

"Hush," she whispered, and at that moment Selwyn emerged into full view. Catching sight of me he stopped in evident surprise.

"I was told I should find Miss Elizabeth here," he said stiffly.

"It would almost appear that you had been misinformed," I answered. For a moment he seemed undecided what to do. Would he go away? I wondered. Evidently not, for after glancing about him he sat himself down upon a rustic seat near-by with a certain resolute air that I did not like. I must get rid of him at all hazards.

"Sir," said I, "can I trespass on your generosity to the extent of a match— or say a couple?" After a brief hesitation he drew out a very neat silver match-box, which he handed to me.

"A fine day, sir?" I said, puffing at my pipe.

Mr. Selwyn made no reply.

"I hear that the crops are looking particularly healthy this year," I went on.

Mr. Selwyn appeared to be utterly lost in the contemplation of an adjacent tree.

"To my mind an old apple tree is singularly picturesque," I began again, "nice nobbly branches, don't you know."

Mr. Selwyn began to fidget.

"And then," I pursued, "they tell me that apples are so good for the blood."

Mr. Selwyn shifted his gaze to the toe of his riding boot, and for a space there was silence, so much so, indeed, that an inquisitive rabbit crept up and sat down to watch us with much interest, until—evidently remembering some pressing engagement—he disappeared with a flash of his white tail.

"Talking of rabbits," said I, "they are quite a pest in Australia, I believe, and are exterminated by the thousand; I have often wondered if a syndicate could not be formed to acquire the skins—this idea, so far as I know, is original, but you are quite welcome to it if——"

Mr. Selwyn rose abruptly to his feet. .

"I once in my boyhood possessed a rabbit—of the lop-eared variety," I continued, "which overate itself and died. I remember I attempted to skin it with dire results——"

"Sir," said Mr. Selwyn, "I beg to inform you that I am not interested in rabbits, lop-eared or otherwise, nor do I propose to become so; further-more——"

But at this moment of my triumph, even as he turned to depart, something small and white fluttered down from the branches above, and the next moment Selwyn had stooped and picked up a lace handkerchief. Then, while he stared at it and I at him, there came a ripple of laughter and Lisbeth peered down at us through the leaves.

"My handkerchief—thank you," she said, as Selwyn stood somewhat taken aback by her sudden appearance.

"The trees hereabouts certainly bear very remarkable, not to say delightful fruit," he said.

"And as you will remember, I was always particularly fond of apple trees," I interpolated.

"Mr. Selwyn," smiled Lisbeth, "let me introduce you to Mr. Brent."

"Sir," said I, "I am delighted to make your acquaintance; have heard Her Grace of Chelsea speak of you— her friends are mine, I trust?"

Mr. Selwyn's bow was rather more than distant.

"I have already had the pleasure of meeting this—this very original gentleman before, and under rather peculiar circumstances, Miss Elizabeth," he said, and forthwith plunged into an account of the whole affair of the "ambushes," while Lisbeth, perched upon her lofty throne, surveyed us with an ever-growing astonishment.

"Whatever does it all mean?" she inquired as Mr. Selwyn made an end.

"You must know, then," I explained, leaning upon my quarter-staff, "the Imp took it into his head to become Robin Hood; I was Little-John, and Mr. Selwyn here was so very obliging as to enact the rôle of Sheriff of Nottingham——"

"I beg your pardon," exclaimed Mr. Selwyn indignantly, turning upon me with a fiery eye.

"Every one recollects the immortal exploits of Robin and his 'merrie men,'" I continued, "and you will, of course, remember that they had a habit of capturing the Sheriff and tying him up to trees and things. Naturally the Imp did not proceed to that extreme. He contented himself with merely capturing the Sheriff's hat—I think that you will agree that those 'ambushes' worked like a charm, Mr. Selwyn?"

"Miss Elizabeth," he said, disdaining any reply, "I am aware of the affection you lavish upon your nephew; I hope that you will take measures to restrain him from such pranks—such very disgraceful pranks—in the future. I myself should suggest a change of companionship [here he glanced at me] as the most salutary

method. Good-afternoon, Miss Elizabeth." So saying, Mr. Selwyn raised
his hat, bowed stiffly to me, and turning upon an indignant heel, strode
haughtily away.

"Well!" exclaimed Lisbeth, with a
look of very real concern.

"Very well, indeed!" I nodded; "we
are alone at last."

"Oh, Dick! but to have offended him
like this!"

"A highly estimable young gentleman," I said, "though deplorably lack-
ing in that saving sense of humour
which——"

"Aunt Agatha seems to think a great
deal of him."

"So I understand," I nodded.

"Only this morning I received a letter from her, in which, among other
things, she pointed out what a very excellent match he would be."

"And what do you think?"

"Oh, I agree with her, of course;

his family dates back ages and ages
before the Conqueror, and he has two
or three estates besides Selwyn Park,
and one in Scotland."

"Do you know, Lisbeth, that reminds
me of another house—not at all big
or splendid, but of great age; a house
which stands not far from the village
of Down, in Kent; a house which is
going to rack and ruin for want of a
mistress. Sometimes, just as evening
comes on, I think it must dream of
the light feet and gentle hands it has
known so many years ago, and feels its
loneliness more than ever."

"Poor old house!" said Lisbeth
softly.

"Yes, a house is very human, Lisbeth,
especially an old one, and feels the
need of that loving care which only a
woman can bestow, just as we do ourselves."

"Dear old house!" said Lisbeth,
more softly than before.

"How much longer must it wait—
when will you come and care for it,
Lisbeth?"

She started, and I thought her cheeks
seemed a trifle pinker than usual as
her eyes met mine.

"Dick," she said wistfully, "I do
wish you would get the ladder; it's
horribly uncomfortable to sit in a tree
for hours and——"

"First of all, Lisbeth, you will forgive the Imp—full and freely, won't
you?"

"He shall go to bed without any tea
whatever."

"That will be rank cruelty, Lisbeth;
remember he is a growing boy."

"And I have been perched up here—
between heaven and earth—all the
afternoon."

"Then why not come down?" I inquired.

"If you will only get the ladder
——"

"If you will just put your right foot in my——"

"I won't!" said Lisbeth.

"As you please," I nodded, and sitting down, mechanically took out my pipe and began to fill it, while she opened her book, frowning. And after she had read very studiously for perhaps two minutes, she drew out and consulted her watch. I did the same.

"A quarter to five!" I said.

Lisbeth glanced down at me with the air of one who is deliberating upon two courses of action, and when at length she spoke, every trace of irritation had vanished completely.

"Dick, I'm awfully hungry."

"So am I," I nodded.

"It *would* be nice to have tea here under the trees, wouldn't it?"

"It would be positively idyllic!" I said.

"Then if you will please find that ladder——"

"If you will promise to forgive the Imp——"

"Certainly not!" she retorted.

"So be it!" I sighed, and sat down again. As I did so she launched her book at me.

"Beast!" she exclaimed.

"Which means that you are ready to descend?" I inquired, rising and depositing the maltreated volume side by side with my pipe on a rustic table near-by; "very good. Place your right foot in——"

"Oh, all right," she said quite pettishly, and next moment I had her in my arms.

"Dick! put me down—at once!"

"One moment, Lisbeth; that boy is a growing boy——"

"And shall go to bed without any tea!" she broke in.

"Very well, then," I said, and reading the purpose in my eyes, she attempted, quite vainly, to turn her head aside.

"You will find it quite useless to struggle, Lisbeth," I warned. "Your only course is to remember that he is a growing boy."

"And you are a brute!" she cried.

"Undoubtedly," I answered, bending my head nearer her petulant lips. "But think of the Imp in bed, lying there, sleepless, tealess, and growing all the while as fast as he can."

Lisbeth surrendered, of course, but my triumph was greatly tempered with disappointment.

"You will then forgive him for the 'ambushes' and cherish him with much tea?" I stipulated, winking away a tress of hair that tickled most provokingly.

"Yes," said Lisbeth.

"And no bed until the usual hour?"

"No," she answered, quite subdued;

"and now please do put me down."
So I sighed and perforce obeyed.

She stood for a moment patting her
rebellious hair into order with deft,
white fingers, looking up at me meanwhile with a laugh in her eyes that
seemed almost a challenge. I took a
hasty step toward her, but as I did so
the Imp hove into view, and the opportunity was lost.

"Hallo, Auntie Lisbeth!" he exclaimed, eyeing her wonderingly; then
his glance wandered round as if in
quest of something.

"How did she do it, Uncle Dick?"
he inquired.

"Do what, my Imp?"

"Why, get out of the tree?" I smiled
and looked at Lisbeth.

"Did she climb down?"

"No," said I, shaking my head.

"Did she—jump down?"

"No, she didn't jump down, my
Imp."

"Well, did she—did she fly down?"

"No, nor fly down—she just came down."

"Yes, but how did she——"

"Reginald," said Lisbeth, "run and tell the maids to bring tea out here—for three."

"Three?" echoed the Imp. "But Dorothy has gone out to tea, you know—is Uncle Dick going to——"

"To be sure, Imp," I nodded.

"Oh, that is fine—hurrah, Little-John!" he cried, and darted off toward the house.

"And you, Lisbeth?" I said, imprisoning her hands, "are you glad also?"

Lisbeth did not speak, yet I was satisfied nevertheless.

III

THE DESPERADOES

FANE COURT stands bowered in trees, with a wide stretch of the greenest of green lawns sloping down to the river stairs.

They are quaint old stairs, with a marble rail and carved balusters, worn and crumbling, yet whose decay is half hid by the kindly green of lichens and mosses; stairs indeed for an idle fellow to dream over on a hot summer's afternoon—and they were, moreover, a favourite haunt of Lisbeth. It was here that I had moored my boat, therefore, and now lay back, pipe in mouth and with a cushion beneath my head, in that blissful state between sleeping and waking.

Now, as I lay, from the blue

wreaths of my pipe I wove me fair fancies:

And lo! the stairs were no longer deserted; there were fine gentlemen, patched and powdered, in silks and satins, with shoe-buckles that flashed in the sun; there were dainty ladies in quilted petticoats and flowered gowns, with most wonderful coiffures; and there was Lisbeth, fairer and daintier than them all, and there, too, was I. And behold how demurely she courtesied and smiled behind her ivory fan! With what a grace I took a pinch of snuff! With what an air I ogled and bowed with hand on heart! Then, somehow, it seemed we were alone, she on the top stair, I on the lower. And standing thus I raised my arms to her with an appealing gesture. Her eyes looked down into mine, the patch quivered at the corner of her scarlet mouth, and there beside it was the dimple. Beneath her petticoat I saw her foot in a little pink satin shoe come slowly toward me and stop again. I watched, scarce breathing, for it seemed my fate hung in the balance. Would she come down to Love and me, or——

"Ship ahoy!" cried a voice, and in that moment my dream vanished. I sighed, and looking round, beheld a head peering at me over the balustrade; a head bound up in a bandanna handkerchief of large pattern and vivid colouring.

"Why, Imp!" I exclaimed. But my surprise abated when he emerged into full view.

About his waist was a broad-buckled belt, which supported a wooden cutlass, two or three murderous wooden daggers and a brace of toy pistols; while upon his legs were a pair of top-boots many sizes too large for him, so that walking required no little care. Yet on the whole his appearance was

decidedly effective. There could be
no mistake—he was a bloodthirsty
pirate!

The Imp is an artist to his grimy fin-
ger-tips.

"Avast, shipmate!" I cried. "How's
the wind?"

"Oh, he exclaimed, falling over his
boots with eagerness, "do take me in
your boat, an' let's be pirates, will you,
Uncle Dick?"

"Well, that depends. Where is your
Auntie Lisbeth?"

"Mr. Selwyn is going to row her and
Dorothy up the river."

"The deuce he is!"

"Yes, an' they won't take me."

"Why not, my Imp?"

" 'Cause they're 'fraid I should upset
the boat. So I thought I'd come an'
ask you to be a pirate, you know. I'll
lend you my best dagger an' one of
my pistols. Will you, Uncle Dick?"

"Come aboard, shipmate, if you are

for Hispaniola, the Tortugas, and the Spanish Main," said I, whereupon he scrambled in, losing a boot overboard in his haste, which necessitated much intricate angling with the boat-hook ere it was recovered.

"They're Peter's, you know," he explained as he emptied out the water. "I took them out of the harness-room; a pirate must have boots, you know, but I'm afraid Peter'll swear."

"Not a doubt of it when he sees them," I said as we pushed off.

"I wish," he began, looking round thoughtfully after a minute or so, "I wish we could get a plank or a yard-arm from somewhere."

"What for, my Imp?"

"Why, don't you remember, pirates always had a plank for people to 'walk,' you know, an' used to 'swing them up to the yard-arm.'"

"You seem to know all about it," I said as I pulled slowly down stream.

"Oh, yes; I read it all in *Scarlet Sam, the Scourge of the South Seas.* Scarlet Sam was fine. He used to stride up and down the quarterdeck an' flourish his cutlass, an' his eyes would roll, an' he'd foam at the mouth, an'——"

"Knock everybody into 'the lee scuppers,' " I put in.

"Yes," cried the Imp in a tone of unfeigned surprise. "How did you know that, Uncle Dick?"

"Once upon a time," I said, as I swung lazily at the sculls, "I was a boy myself, and read a lot about a gentleman named 'Beetle-browed Ben.' I tell you, Imp, he was a terror for foaming and stamping, if you like, and used to kill three or four people every morning, just to get an appetite for breakfast." The Imp regarded me with round eyes.

"How fine!" he breathed, hugging himself in an ecstasy.

"It was," I nodded; "and then he was a very wonderful man in other ways. You see, he was always getting himself shot through the head, or run through the body, but it never hurt Beetle-browed Ben—not a bit of it."

"An' did he 'swing people at the y a r d - a r m — w i t h a bitter smile'?"

"Lots of 'em!" I answered.

"An' make them 'walk the plank—with a horrid laugh'?"

"By the hundred!"

"An' 'maroon them on a desolate island—with a low chuckle'?"

"Many a time," I answered; "and generally with a chuckle."

"Oh, I should like to read about him!" said the Imp with a deep sigh; "will you lend me your book about him, Uncle Dick?"

I shook my head. "Unfortunately, that, together with many other valued possessions, has been ravaged from me by the ruthless maw of Time," I replied sadly.

The Imp sat plunged in deep thought, trailing his fingers pensively in the water.

"And so your Auntie Lisbeth is going for a row with Mr. Selwyn, is she?" I said.

"Yes, an' I told her she could come an' be a pirate with me if she liked— but she wouldn't."

"Strange!" I murmured.

"Uncle Dick, do you think Auntie Lisbeth is in love with Mr. Selwyn?"

"What?" I exclaimed, and stopped rowing.

"I mean, do you think Mr. Selwyn is in love with Auntie Lisbeth?"

"My Imp, I'm afraid he is. Why?"

" 'Cause cook says he is, an' so does Jane, an' they know all about love, you know. I've heard them read it

out of a book lots an' lots of times.
But I think love is awfull' silly, don't
you, Uncle Dick?"

"Occasionally I greatly fear so," I
sighed.

"You wouldn't go loving anybody,
would you, Uncle Dick?"

"Not if I could help it," I answered,
shaking my head; "but I do love some
one, and that's the worst of it."

"Oh!" exclaimed the Imp, but in a
tone more of sorrow than anger.

"Don't be too hard on me, Imp," I
said; "your turn may come when you
are older; you may love somebody
one of these days."

The Imp frowned and shook his
head. "No," he answered sternly;
"when I grow up big I shall keep fer-
rets. Ben, the gardener's boy, has
one with the littlest, teeniest pink nose
you ever saw."

"Certainly a ferret has its advan-
tages, I mused. "A ferret will not

frown upon one one minute and flash a dimple at one the next. And then, again, a ferret cannot be reasonably supposed to possess an aunt. There is something to be said for your idea after all, Imp."

"Why, then, let's be pirates, Uncle Dick," he said with an air of finality. "I think I'll be Scarlet Sam, 'cause I know all about him, an' you can be Timothy Bone, the boatswain."

"Aye, aye, sir," I responded promptly; "only I say, Imp, don't roll your eyes so frightfully or you may roll yourself overboard."

Scorning reply, he drew his cutlass, and setting it between his teeth in most approved pirate fashion, sat, pistol in hand, frowning terrifically at creation in general.

"Starboard your helm—starboard!" he cried, removing his weapon for the purpose.

"Starboard it is!" I answered.

"Clear away for action!" growled the Imp. "Double-shot the cannonades, and bo'sun, pipe all hands to quarters."

Hereupon I executed a lively imitation of a boatswain's whistle.

Most children are blessed with imagination, but the Imp in this respect is gifted beyond his years. For him there is no such thing as "pretence"; he has but to close his eyes a moment to open them upon a new and a very real world of his own—the golden world of Romance, wherein so few of us are privileged to walk in these cold days of common-sense. And yet it is a very fair world, peopled with giants and fairies; where castles lift their grim, embattled towers; where magic woods and forests cast their shade, full of strange beasts; where knights ride forth with lance in rest and their armour shining in the sun. And right well we know them. There is Roland,

Sir William Wallace, and Hereward
the Wake; Ivanhoe, the Black Knight,
and bold Robin Hood. There is
Amyas Leigh, old Salvation Yeo, and
that lovely rascal Long John Silver.
And there, too, is King Arthur, with
his Knights of the Round Table—but
the throng is very great, and who
could name them all?

So the Imp and I sailed away into
this wonderful world of romance
aboard our gallant vessel, which, like
any other pirate ship that ever existed
—in books or out of them—"luffed,
and filling upon another tack, stood
away in pursuit of the Spanish treasure galleon in the offing."

What pen could justly describe the
fight which followed—how guns
roared and pistols flashed, while the
air was full of shouts and cries and the
thundering din of battle; how Scarlet
Sam foamed and stamped and flourished his cutlass; how Timothy Bone

piped his whistle as a bo'sun should?
We had already sunk five great gal-
leons and were hard at work with a
sixth, which was evidently in a bad
way, when Scarlet Sam ceased foaming
and pointed over my shoulder with his
dripping blade.

"Sail ho!" he cried.

"Where away?" I called back.

"Three points on the weather bow."
As he spoke came the sound of oars,
and turning my head, I saw a skiff
approaching, sculled by a man in
irreproachable flannels and straw
hat.

"Why, it's—it's him!" cried the Imp
suddenly. "Heave to, there!" he bellowed in the voice of Scarlet Sam.
"Heave to, or I'll sink you with a
'murderous broadside!'" Almost
with the words, and before I could
prevent him, he gave a sharp tug to
the rudder lines; there was an angry
exclamation behind me, a shock, a

splintering of wood, and I found myself face to face with Mr. Selwyn, flushed and hatless.

"Damn!" said Mr. Selwyn, and proceeded to fish for his hat with the shaft of his broken oar.

The Imp sat for a moment half frightened at his handiwork, then rose to his feet, cutlass in hand, but I punted him gently back into his seat with my foot.

"Really," I began, "I'm awfully sorry, you know—er——"

"May I inquire," said Mr. Selwyn cuttingly, as he surveyed his dripping hat—"may I inquire how it all happened?"

"A most deplorable accident, I assure you. If I can tow you back I shall be delighted, and as for the damage——"

"The damage is trifling, thanks," he returned icily; "it is the delay that I find annoying."

"You have my very humblest apologies," I said meekly. "If I can be of any service——" Mr. Selwyn stopped me with a wave of his hand.

"Thank you, I think I can manage," he said; "but I should rather like to know how it happened. You are unused to rowing, I presume?"

"Sir," I answered, "it was chiefly owing to the hot-headedness of Scarlet Sam, the Scourge of the South Seas."

"I beg your pardon?" said Mr. Selwyn with raised brows.

"Sir," I went on, "at this moment you probably believe yourself to be Mr. Selwyn of Selwyn Park. Allow me to dispel that illusion; you are, on the contrary, Don Pedro Vasquez da Silva, commanding the *Esmeralda* galleasse, bound out of Santa Crux. In us you behold Scarlet Sam and Timothy Bone, of the good ship

Black Death, with the 'skull and cross-bones' fluttering at our peak. If you don't see it, that is not our fault."

Mr. Selwyn stared at me in wide-eyed astonishment, then shrugging his shoulders, turned his back upon me and paddled away as best he might.

"Well, Imp," I said, "you've done it this time!"

" 'Fraid I have," he returned; "but oh! wasn't it grand—and all that about Don Pedro an' the treasure galleon! I do wish I knew as much as you do, Uncle Dick. I'd be a real pirate then."

"Heaven forfend!" I exclaimed.

So I presently turned and rowed back upstream, not a little perturbed in my mind as to the outcome of the adventure.

"Not a word, mind!" I cautioned as I caught sight of a certain dainty figure watching our approach from the shade of her parasol. The Imp nodded, sighed, and sheathed his cutlass.

"Well!" said Lisbeth as we glided up to the water-stairs; "I wonder what mischief you have been after together?"

"We have been floating upon a river of dreams," I answered, rising and lifting my hat; "we have likewise discoursed of many things. In the words of the immortal Carroll:

" 'Of shoes, and ships, and sealing wax, and cabbages, and——' "

"Pirates!" burst out the Imp.

"This dream river of ours," I went on, quelling him with a glance, "has carried us to you, which is very right and proper. Dream rivers always should, more especially when you sit

" ' 'Mid sunshine throned, and all alone.' "

"But I'm not all alone, Dick."

"No; I'm here," said a voice, and Dorothy appeared with her small and very fluffy kitten under her arm as usual. "We are waiting for Mr. Selwyn, you know. We've waited, oh! a long, long time, but he hasn't come, and Auntie says he's a beast, and——"

"Dorothy!" exclaimed Lisbeth, frowning.

"Yes, you did, Auntie," said Dorothy, nodding her head. "I heard you when Louise ran up a tree and I had to coax her back; and I have a clean frock on, too, and Louise will be oh so disappointed!" Here she kissed the fluffy kitten on the nose. "So he is a beast; don't you think so, Uncle Dick?"

"Such delay is highly reprehensible," I nodded.

"I'm glad you've come, Uncle Dick, and so is Auntie. She was hoping——"

"That will do, Dorothy!" Lisbeth interrupted.

"I wonder what she was hoping?" I sighed.

"If you say another word, Dorothy, I won't tell you any more about the Fairy Prince," said Lisbeth.

"Why, then," I continued, seeing the threat had the desired effect, "since Mr. Selwyn hasn't turned up, perhaps you would care to——"

—"Be a pirate?" put in the Imp.

"To come for a row with us?" I corrected.

—"Aboard the good ship *Black Death*," he went on, " 'with the skull an' cross-bones at our peak.' "

"Thanks," said Lisbeth, "but really, I don't think I should. What a horrible name!"

"What's in a name? a boat by any other—" I misquoted. "If you like, we'll call it the *Joyful Hope*, bound for the Land of Heart's Delight."

Lisbeth shook her head, but I fancied the dimple peeped at me for a moment.

"It would be a pity to disappoint Louise," I said, reaching up to stroke the fluffy kitten.

"Yes," cried Dorothy, "do let's go, Auntie."

"For the sake of Louise," I urged, and held out my arms to her. Lisbeth was standing on the top stair and I on the lower, in exactly the same attitudes as I had beheld in my vision. I saw her foot come slowly toward me and stop again; her red lips quivered into a smile, and lo, there was the dimple! Dorothy saw it, too—children are wonderfully quick in such matters—and next moment was ensconced in the boat, Louise in her lap, and there was nothing left for Lisbeth but to follow.

The Imp went forward to keep a "lookout," and finding a length of

fishing line, announced his intention
of "heaving the lead."

I have upon several occasions ridden
with Lisbeth—she is a good horse-
woman—frequently danced with her,
but never before had I been with her
in a boat. The novelty of it was
therefore decidedly pleasing, the more
so as she sat so close that by furtively
reaching out a foot I could just touch
the hem of her dress.

"Uncle Dick," said Dorothy, looking up at me with her big grey eyes,
"where is the Land of Heart's Delight?"

"It lies beyond the River of
Dreams," I answered.

"Is it far away?"

"I'm afraid it is, Dorothy."

"Oh!—and hard to get to?"

"Yes; though it depends altogether
upon who is at the helm."

Lisbeth very slowly began to tie a
knot in the rudder-line.

"Well, Auntie's steering now. Could she get us there?"

"Yes, she could get us there, if she would."

"Oh!" cried Dorothy, "do—do steer for the Land of Heart's Delight, Auntie Lisbeth; it sounds so pretty, and I'm sure Louise would like it ever so much."

But Lisbeth only laughed, and tied another knot in the rudder-line.

"The Land of Heart's Delight!" repeated Dorothy. "It sounds rather like Auntie's tale of the Fairy Prince. His name was Trueheart."

"And what was Prince Trueheart like?" I inquired.

"Fine!" broke in the Imp. "He used to fight dragons, you know."

"And he lived in a palace of crystal," continued Dorothy, "and he was so good and kind that the birds used to make friends with him!"

"An' he wore gold armour, an' a

big feather in his helmet!" supplemented the Imp.

"And of course he loved the beautiful princess," I ended.

"Yes," nodded Dorothy; "but how did you know there was a beautiful princess?"

"Uncle Dick knows everything, of course," returned the Imp sententiously.

"Do you think the beautiful princess loved the prince, Dorothy?"I asked, glancing at Lisbeth's averted face.

"Well," answered Dorothy, pursing her mouth thoughtfully, "I don't know, Uncle Dick; you see, Auntie hasn't got to that yet, but everybody loves somebody sometime, you know. Betty—she's our cook, you know— Betty says all nice tales end up in marrying and living happy ever after."

"Not a doubt of it," said I, resting on my oars. "What do you think, Lisbeth?" She leaned back and regarded me demurely beneath her long lashes for a moment.

"I think," she answered, "that it would be much nicer if you would go on rowing."

"One more question," I said. "Tell me, has this Prince Trueheart got a moustache?"

"Like Mr. Selwyn?" cried the Imp; "should think not. The prince was a fine chap, an' used to kill dragons, you know."

"Ah! I'm glad of that," I murmured, passing my fingers across my shaven upper lip; "very glad indeed." Lisbeth laughed, but I saw her colour deepen and she looked away.

"Oh, it must be lovely to kill a dragon!" sighed the Imp.

Now, as he spoke, chancing to look round, I saw in the distance a man in a boat, who rowed most lustily—and the man wore a Panama.

Hereupon, taking a fresh grip upon

my long sculls, I began to row—to row, indeed, as I had not done for many a year, with a long, steady stroke that made the skiff fairly leap.

Who does not know that feeling of exhilaration as the blades grip the water and the gentle lapping at the bow swells into a gurgling song?" The memorable time when I had "stroked" Cambridge to victory was nothing to this. Then it was but empty glory that hung in the balance, while now——!

I settled my feet more firmly, and lengthening my stroke, pulled with a will. Lisbeth sat up, and I saw her fingers tighten upon the rudder-lines.

"You asked me to row, you know," I said in response to her look.

"Yo ho!" roared Scarlet Sam in the gruffest of nautical tones. "By the deep nine, an' the wind's a-lee, so heave, my mariners all—O!"

At first we began to gain considerably upon our pursuer, but presently I saw him turn his head, saw the Panama tossed aside as Mr. Selwyn settled down to real business—and the struggle began.

Very soon, probably owing to the fixedness of my gaze, or my unremitting exertion, or both, Lisbeth seemed to become aware of the situation, and turned to look over her shoulder. I set my teeth as I waited to meet her indignant look, for I had determined to continue the struggle, come what might. But when at last she did confront me her eyes were shining, her cheeks were flushed and there actually was—the dimple.

"Sit still, children," she said, and that was all; but for one moment her eyes looked into mine.

The old river has witnessed many a hard-fought race in its time, but never was there one more hotly contested than this. Never was the song of the water more pleasant to my ear, never was the spring and bend of the long sculls more grateful, as the banks swept by faster and faster. No pirate straining every inch of canvas to escape well-merited capture, no smuggler fleeing for some sheltered cove, with the revenue cutter close astern, ever experienced a keener excitement than did we.

The Imp was in a perfect ecstasy of delight; even Dorothy forgot her beloved Louise for the time, while Lisbeth leaner toward me, the tiller-lines over her shoulders, her lips parted and a light in her eyes I had never seen there before. And yet Selwyn hung fast in our rear. If he was deficient in a sense of humour, he could certainly row.

"He was an Oxford Blue," said Lisbeth, speaking almost in a whisper, "and he has an empty boat!"

I longed to kiss the point of her little tan shoe or the hem of her dress for those impulsive words, and tried to tell her so with my eyes—breath was too precious just then. Whether she understood or not I won't be sure, but I fancy she did from the way her lashes drooped.

"Oh, my eyes!" bellowed Scarlet Sam; "keep her to it, quartermaster, an' take a turn at the mizzen-shrouds!"

When I again glanced at our pursuer I saw that he was gaining. Yes, there could be no mistake; slowly but surely, try as I would, the distance between us lessened and lessened, until he was so near that I could discern the very parting of his back hair. So, perforce, bowing to the inevitable, I ceased my exertions, contenting myself with a long, easy stroke. Thus by the time he was alongside I had in some measure recovered my breath.

"Miss—Eliz—beth," he panted, very hot of face and moist of brow, "must beg—the—favour—of few words with you."

"With pleasure, Mr. Selwyn," answered Lisbeth, radiant with smiles; "as many as you wish." Forthwith Mr. Selwyn panted out his indictment against the desperadoes of the *Black Death,* while the Imp glanced apprehensively from him to Lisbeth and stole his hand furtively into mine.

"I should not have troubled you with this, Miss Elizabeth," Selwyn ended, "but that I would not have you think me neglectful of an appointment, especially with you."

"Indeed, Mr. Selwyn, I am very grateful to you for opening my eyes to such a—a——"

"Very deplorable accident," I put in.

"I—I was perfectly certain," she continued, without so much as glancing in my direction, "that you would

never have kept me waiting without
sufficient reason. And now, Mr.
Brent, if you will be so obliging as to
take us to the bank, Mr. Selwyn shall
row us back—if he will."

"Delighted!" he murmured.

"I ordered tea served in the orchard
at five o'clock," smiled Lisbeth, "and
it is only just four, so——"

"Which bank would you prefer," I
inquired—"the right or the left?"

"The nearest," said Lisbeth.

"Which should you think was the
nearest, Mr. Selwyn?" I queried.

Disdaining any reply, Selwyn ran his
skiff ashore, and I obediently followed. Without waiting for my assistance, Lisbeth deftly made the exchange from one boat to the other,
followed more slowly by Dorothy.

"Come, Reginald," she said, as Selwyn made ready to push off; "we're
waiting for you!" The Imp squatted
closer to me.

"Reginald Augustus!" said Lisbeth. The Imp shuffled uneasily.

"Are you coming?" inquired Lisbeth.

"I—I'd rather be a pirate with Uncle Dick, please, Auntie Lisbeth," he said at last.

"Very well," nodded Lisbeth with an air of finality; "then of course I must punish you." But her tone was strangely gentle, and as she turned away I'll swear I saw the ghost of that dimple—yes, I'll swear it.

So we sat very lonely and dejected, the Imp and I, desperadoes though we were, as we watched Selwyn's boat grow smaller and smaller until it was lost round a bend in the river.

" 'Spect I shall get sent to bed for this," said the Imp after a long pause.

"I think it more than probable, my Imp."

"But then, it was a very fine race— oh, beautiful!" he sighed; "an' I couldn't desert my ship an' Timothy

" Disdaining any reply, Selwyn ran his skiff ashore "

Bone, an' leave you here all by yourself—now could I, Uncle Dick?"

"Of course not, Imp."

"What are you thinking about,
Uncle Dick?" he inquired as I stared,
chin in hand, at nothing in particular.

"I was wondering, Imp, where the
River of Dreams was going to lead
me, after all."

"To the Land of Heart's Delight,
of course," he answered promptly;
"you said so, you know, an' you never
tell lies, Uncle Dick—never."

IV

MOON MAGIC

THE Three Jolly Anglers is an inn of
a distinctly jovial aspect, with its top-
pling gables, its creaking sign, and its
bright lattices, which, like merry little twinkling eyes, look down upon
the eternal river to-day with the same
half-waggish, half-kindly air as they
have done for generations.

Upon its battered sign, if you look
closely enough, you may still see the
Three Anglers themselves, somewhat
worn and dim with time and stress of
weather, yet preserving their jollity
through it all with an heroic fortitude
—as they doubtless will do until they
fade away altogether.

It is an inn with raftered ceilings,
and narrow, winding passageways; an

inn with long, low chambers full of
unexpected nooks and corners, with
great four-post beds built for tired
giants it would seem, and wide, deep
chimneys reminiscent of Gargantuan
rounds of beef; an inn whose very
walls seem to exude comfort, as it
were—the solid comfortable comfort
of a bygone age.

Of all the many rooms here to be
found I love best that which is called
the Sanded Parlour. Never were
wainscoted walls of a mellower tone,
never was pewter more gleaming,
never were things more bright and
speckless, from the worn, quaint andirons on the hearth to the brass-
bound blunderbuss, with the two ancient fishing-rods above. At one end
of the room was a long, low casement,
and here I leaned, watching the river
near-by, and listening to its never-ceas-
ing murmur. I had dined an hour
ago; the beef had been excellent—it

always is at the Three Jolly Anglers
—and the ale beyond all criticism;
also my pipe seemed to have an added
flavour.

Yet despite all this I did not enjoy
that supreme content—that philosoph-
ical calm which such beef and such ale
surely warranted. But then, who ever
heard of Love and Philosophy going
together?

Away over the uplands a round, har-
vest moon was beginning to rise,
flecking the shadowy waters with
patches of silver, and, borne to my ears
upon the warm, still air, came the
throb of distant violins. This served
only to deepen my melancholy, re-
minding me that somebody or other
was giving a ball to-night; and Lisbeth was there, and Mr. Selwyn was
there, of course, and I—I was here—
alone with the brass-bound blunderbuss, the ancient fishing-rods and the
antique andirons on the hearth; with

none to talk to save the moon, and the jasmine that had crept in at the open casement. And noting the splendour of the night, I experienced towards Lisbeth a feeling of pained surprise, that she should prefer the heat and garish glitter of a ball-room to walking beneath such a moon with me.

Indeed, it was a wondrous night! one of those warm, still nights which seem full of vague and untold possibilities! A night with magic in the air, when elves and fairies dance within their grassy rings, or hiding amid the shade of trees, peep out at one between the leaves; or again, some gallant knight on mighty steed may come pacing slowly from the forest shadows, with the moonlight bright upon his armour.

Yes, surely there was magic in the air to-night! I half wished that some enchanter might, by a stroke of his fairy wand, roll back the years and

leave me in the brutal, virile, Good
Old Times, when men wooed and won
their loves by might and strength of
arm, and not by gold, as is so often
the case in these days of ours. To be
mounted upon my fiery steed, lance in
hand and sword on thigh, riding down
the leafy alleys of the woods yonder,
led by the throbbing, sighing melody.
To burst upon the astonished dancers
like a thunder-clap; to swing her up
to my saddle-bow, and clasped in each
other's arms, to plunge into the green
mystery of forest.

My fancies had carried me thus far
when I became aware of a small, furtive figure, dodging from one patch
of shadow to another. Leaning from
the window, I made out the form of
a somewhat disreputable urchin, who,
dropping upon hands and knees, proceeded to crawl towards me over the
grass with a show of the most elaborate caution.

"Hallo!" I exclaimed, "halt and give the counter-sign!" The urchin sat up on his heels and stared at me with a pair of very round, bright eyes.

"Please, are you Mr. Uncle Dick?" he inquired.

"Oh," I said, "you come from the Imp, I presume." The boy nodded a round head, at the same time fumbling with something in his pocket.

"And whom may you be?" I inquired, conversationally.

"I'm Ben, I am."

"The gardener's boy?" Again the round head nodded acquiescence, as with much writhing and twisting he succeeded in drawing a heterogeneous collection of articles from his pocket, whence he selected a very dirty and crumpled piece of paper.

"He wants a ladder so's he can git out, but it's too big fer me to lift, so he told me to give you this here so's you would come an' rescue him—

please, Mr. Uncle Dick." With which lucid explanation Ben handed me the crumpled note.

Spreading it out upon the window-sill, I managed to make out as follows:

DEAR UNKEL DICK: I'm riting this with my hart's blood bekors I'm a prisner in a gloomie dungun. It isn't really my hart's blood it's only red ink, so don't worry. Aunty lisbath cent me to bed just after tea bekors she said i'm norty, and when she'd gone Nurse locked me in so i can't get out and i'm tired of being a prisner, so please i want you to get the ladda and let me eskape, please unkel dick, will you.

yours till deth,
REGINALD AUGUSTUS.

Auntie was reading Ivanhoe to us and i've been the Black Knight and you can be Gurth the swine-herd if you like.

"So that's the way of it?" I said.

"Well! well! such an appeal shall not go unanswered, at least. Wait there, my trusty Benjamin, and I'll be with you anon." Pausing only to refill my tobacco-pouch and get my cap, I sallied out into the fragrant night, and set off along the river, the faithful Benjamin trotting at my heels.

Very soon we were skirting blooming flower-beds, and crossing trim lawns, until at length we reached a certain wing of the house from a window of which a pillow-case was dangling by means of a string.

"That's for provisions!" volunteered Ben; "we pertended he was starving, so he lets it down an' I fill it with onions out of the vegetable garden." At this moment the curly head of the Imp appeared at the window, followed by the major portion of his person.

"Oh, Uncle Dick!" he cried in a loud stage-whisper, "I think you had

MY LADY CAPRICE

better be the Black Knight, 'cause
you're so big, you know."

"Imp," I said, "get in at once, do
you want to break your neck?"
The Imp obediently wriggled into
safety.

"The ladder's in the tool-house,
Uncle Dick—Ben'll show you. Will
you get it, please?" he pleaded in a
wheedling tone.

"First of all, my Imp, why did your
Auntie Lisbeth send you to bed—had
you been a very naughty boy?"

"No-o!" he answered, after a moment's pause, "I don't think I was so
very naughty—I only painted Dorothy like an Indian chief—green, with
red spots, an' she looked fine, you
know."

"Green, with red spots!" I repeated.

"Yes; only auntie didn't seem to like
it."

. "I fear your Auntie Lisbeth lacks an
eye for colour."

"Yes, 'fraid so; she sent me to bed for it, you know."

"Still, Imp, under the circumstances I think it would be best if you got undressed and went to sleep."

"Oh, but I can't, Uncle Dick!"

"Why not, my Imp?"

" 'Cause the moon's so very bright, an' everything looks so fine down there, an' I'm sure there's fairies about—Moon-fairies, you know, and I'm miserable."

"Miserable, Imp?"

"Yes, Auntie Lisbeth never came to kiss me good-night, an' so I can't go to sleep, Uncle Dick!"

"Why that alters the case, certainly."

"Yes, an' the ladder's in the tool-house."

"Imp," I said, as I turned to follow Benjamin, "oh, you Imp!" There are few things in this world more difficult to manage than a common or garden ladder; among other peculiarities it has a most unpleasant knack of kicking out suddenly just as everything appears to be going smoothly, which is apt to prove disconcerting to the novice. However, after sundry mishaps of the kind, I eventually got it reared up to the window, and a moment afterwards the Imp had climbed down and stood beside me, drawing the breath of freedom.

As a precautionary measure we proceeded to hide the ladder in a clump of rhododendrons hard by, and had but just done so when Benjamin uttered a cry of warning and took to his heels, while the Imp and I sought shelter behind a friendly tree. And not a whit too soon, for, scarcely had we done so, when two figures came round a corner of the house—two figures who walked very slowly and very close together.

"Why it's Betty—the cook, you

know—an' Peter!" whispered the
Imp.

Almost opposite our hiding-place
Betty paused to sigh heavily and stare
up at the moon.

"Oh, Peter!" she murmured, "look
at that there orb!"

"Ar!" said Peter, gazing obediently
upward.

"Peter, ain't it 'eavenly; don't it stir
your very soul?"

"Ar!" said Peter.

"Peter, are you sure you loves me
more than that Susan thing at the
doctor's?" A corduroy coat-sleeve
crept slowly about Betty's plump
waist, and there came the unmistakable sound of a kiss.

"Really and truly, Peter?"

"Ar!" said Peter, "so 'elp me Sam!"
The kissing sound was repeated, and
they walked on once more, only closer
than ever now on account of the corduroy coat-sleeve.

"Those two are in love, you know,"
nodded the Imp. "Peter says the
cheese-cakes she makes are enough to
drive any man into marrying her,
whether he wants to or not, an' I
heard Betty telling Jane that she
adored Peter, 'cause he had so much
soul! Why is it," he inquired, thoughtfully, as he watched the two out of
sight, "why is it, Uncle Dick, that
people in love always look so silly?"

"Do you think so?" I asked, as I
paused to light my pipe.

"'Course I do!" returned the Imp;
"what's any one got to put their arm
round girls for, just as if they wanted
holding up—I think it's awfull'
silly!"

"Of course it is, Imp—your wisdom
is unassailable—still, do you know, I
can understand a man being foolish
enough to do it—occasionally."

"But you never would, Uncle Dick?"

"Alas, Imp!" I said, shaking my

head, "Fortune seems to preclude all chances of it."

"'Course you wouldn't," he exclaimed; "an' Ivanhoe wouldn't——"

"Ah, but he did!" I put in; "have you forgotten Rowena?"

"Oh!" cried the Imp dolefully, "do you really think he ever put his arm round her?"

"Sure of it," I nodded. The Imp seemed much cast down, and even shocked.

"But there was the Black Knight," he said, brightening suddenly—"Richard of the Lion Heart, you know— he never did!"

"Not while he was fighting, of course, but afterwards, if history is to be believed, he very frequently did; and we are all alike, Imp—everybody does sooner or later."

"But why? Why should any one want to put their arm round a girl, Uncle Dick?"

"For the simple reason that the girl is there to put it round, I suppose. And now, Imp, let us talk of fish."

Instinctively we had wandered towards the river, and now we stood to watch the broad, silver path made by the moon across the mystery of its waters.

"I love to see the shine upon the river like that," said the Imp, dreamily;" Auntie Lisbeth says it's the path that the Moon-fairies come down by to bring you nice dreams when you've been good. I've got out of bed lots of times an' watched an' watched, but I've never seen them come. Do you think there are fairies in the moon, Uncle Dick?"

"Undoubtedly," I answered; "how else does it keep so bright? I used to wonder once how they managed to make it shine so."

"It must need lots of rubbing!" said

the Imp; "I wonder if they ever get tired?"

"Of course they do, Imp, and disheartened, too, sometimes, like the rest of us, and then everything is black, and people wonder where the moon is. But they are very brave, these Moon-fairies, and they never quite lose hope, you know; so they presently go back to their rubbing and polishing, always starting at one edge. And in a little while we see it begin to shine again, very small and thin at first, like a——"

"Thumb-nail!"

"Yes, just like a thumb-nail; and so they go on working and working at it until it gets as big and round and bright as it is tonight."

Thus we walked together through a fairy world, the Imp and I, while above the murmur of the waters, above the sighing of the trees, came the soft, tremulous melody of the violins.

"I do wish I had lived when there were knights like Ivanhoe," burst out the Imp suddenly; "it must have been fine to knock a man off his horse with your lance."

"Always supposing he didn't knock you off first, Imp."

"Oh! I should have been the sort of knight that nobody could knock off, you know. An' I'd have wandered about on my faithful charger, fighting all sorts of caddish barons, and caitiffs, an' slaying giants; an' I'd have rescued lovely ladies from castles grim —though I wouldn't have put my arm round them, of course!"

"Perish the thought, my Imp!"

"Uncle Dick!" he said, insinuatingly, "I do wish you'd be the Black Knight, an' let me be Ivanhoe."

"But there are no caitiffs and things left for us to fight, Imp, and no lovely ladies to rescue from castles grim, alas!"

Now we had been walking on, drawn almost imperceptibly by the magic thread of the melody, which had led us, by devious paths, to a low stone wall, beyond which we could see the gleam of lighted windows and the twinkle of fairy-lamps among the trees. And over there, amid the music and laughter, was Lisbeth in all the glory of her beauty, happy, of course, and light-hearted; and here, beneath the moon, was I.

"We could pretend this was a castle grim, you know, Uncle Dick, full of dungeons an' turrets, an' that we were going to rescue Auntie Lisbeth."

"Imp," I said, "that's really a great idea."

"I wish I'd brought my trusty sword," he sighed, searching about for something to supply its place; "I left it under my pillow, you know."

Very soon, however, he had procured
two sticks, somewhat thin and wobbly,
yet which, by the magic of imagination, became transformed into formidable, two-edged swords, with one of
which he armed me, the other he flourished above his head.

"Forward, gallant knights!" he
cried; "the breach! the breach! On!
on! St. George, for Merrie Eng-
land!" With the words he clambered
upon the wall and disappeared upon
the other side.

For a moment I hesitated, and
then, inspired by the music and the
thought of Lisbeth, I followed suit.
It was all very mad, of course, but
who cared for sanity on such a night
—certainly not I.

"Careful now, Imp!" I cautioned;
"if any one should see us they'll take
us for thieves, or lunatics, beyond a
doubt."

We found ourselves in an enclosed

garden with a walk which led between rows of fruit trees. Following this, it brought us out upon a broad stretch of lawn, with here and there a great tree, and beyond, the gleaming windows of the house. Filled with the spirit of adventure, we approached, keeping in the shadow as much as possible, until we could see figures that strolled to and fro upon the terrace or promenaded the walks below.

The excitement of dodging our way among so many people was intense; time and again we were only saved from detection by more than one wandering couple, owing to the fact that all their attention was centred in themselves. For instance, we were skirmishing round a clump of laurels, to gain the shadow of the terrace, when we almost ran into the arms of a pair; but they didn't see us for the very good reason that she was staring at the moon, and he at her.

"So sweet of you, Archibald!" she was saying.

"What did she call him 'bald for, Uncle Dick?" inquired the Imp in a loud stage-whisper, as I dragged him down behind the laurels. 'He's not a bit bald, you know! An' I say, Uncle Dick, did you see his arm, it was round——"

"Yes—yes!" I nodded.

"Just like Peter's, you know."

"Yes—yes, I saw."

"I wonder why she called him——"

"Hush!" I broke in, "his name is Archibald, I suppose."

"Well, I hope when I grow up nobody will ever call me——"

"Hush!" I said again, "not a word —there's your Auntie Lisbeth! She was, indeed, standing upon the terrace, within a yard of our hiding-place, and beside her was Mr. Selwyn.

"Uncle Dick," whispered the irrepressible Imp, "do you think if we

watch long enough that Mr. Selwyn
will put his arm round——"

"Shut up!" I whispered savagely.

Lisbeth was clad in a long, trailing
gown of dove-coloured silk—one of
those close-fitting garments that make
the uninitiated, such as myself, wonder how they are ever got on. Also,
she wore a shawl, which I was sorry
for, because I have always been an ad-
mirer of beautiful things, and Lisbeth's neck and shoulders are glorious.

Mr. Selwyn stood beside her with a
plate of ice cream in his hand, which
he handed to her, and they sat down.
As I watched her and noticed her
weary, bored air, and how wistfully
she gazed up at the silver disc of the
moon, I experienced a feeling of de-
cided satisfaction.

"Yes," said Lisbeth, toying absently
with the ice cream, "he painted Dorothy's face with stripes of red and
green enamel, and goodness only

knows how we can ever get it all
off!"

Mr. Selwyn was duly shocked and
murmured something about 'the ef-
ficacy of turpentine' in such an emer-
gency.

"Of course, I had to punish him,"
continued Lisbeth, "so I sent him to
bed immediately after tea, and never
went to say good-night, or tuck him
up as I usually do, and it has been
worrying me all the evening."

Mr. Selwyn was sure that he was all
right, and positively certain that at
this moment he was wrapped in balmy
slumber. Despite my warning grasp,
the Imp chuckled, but we were saved
by the band striking up. Mr. Selwyn
rose, giving his arm to Lisbeth, and
they re-entered the ball-room. One
by one the other couples followed suit
until the long terrace was deserted.

Now, upon Lisbeth's deserted chair,
showing wonderfully pink in the soft

glow of the Chinese lanterns, was the ice cream.

"Uncle Dick," said the Imp in his thoughtful way, "I think I'll be a bandit for a bit."

"Anything you like," I answered rashly, "so long as we get away while we can."

"All right," he whispered, "I won't be a minute," and before I could stop him he had scrambled down the steps and fallen to upon the ice cream.

The wonderful celerity with which the Imp wolfed down that ice cream was positively awe-inspiring. In less time almost than it takes to tell the plate was empty. Yet scarcely had he swallowed the last mouthful when he heard Mr. Selwyn's voice close by. In his haste the Imp dropped his cap, a glaring affair of red and white, and before he could recover it Lisbeth reappeared, followed by Mr. Selwyn.

—"It certainly is more pleasant out here!" he was saying.

Lisbeth came straight towards the cap—it was a moral impossibility that she could fail to see it—yet she sank into her chair without word or sign. Mr. Selwyn, on the contrary, stood with the empty ice plate in his hand, staring at it in wide-eyed astonishment.

"It's gone!" he exclaimed.

"Oh!" said Lisbeth.

"Most extraordinary!" said Mr. Selwyn, fixing his monocle and staring harder than ever; "I wonder where it can have got to?"

"Perhaps it melted!" Lisbeth suggested, "and I should so have loved an ice!" she sighed.

"Then, of course, I'll get you another, with pleasure," he said and hurried off, eyeing the plate dubiously as he went.

No sooner was Lisbeth alone than

she kicked aside the train of her dress and picked up the tell-tale cap.

"Imp!" she whispered, rising to her feet, "Imp, come here at once, sir!" There was a moment's breathless pause, and then the Imp squirmed himself into view.

"Hallo, Auntie Lisbeth!" he said, with a cheerfulness wholly assumed.

"Oh!" she cried, distressfully, "whatever does this mean; what are you doing here? Oh, you naughty boy!"

"Lisbeth," I said, as I rose in my turn and confronted her, "do not blame the child—the fault is mine—let me explain; by means of a ladder——"

"Not here," she whispered, glancing nervously towards the ball-room.

"Then come where I can."

"Impossible!"

"Not at all; you have only to descend these steps and we can talk undisturbed."

"Ridiculous!" she said, stooping to replace the Imp's cap; but being thus temptingly within reach, she was next moment beside us in the shadows.

"Dick, how could you, how dared you?"

"You see, I had to explain," I answered very humbly; "I really couldn't allow this poor child to bear the blame of my fault——"

"I'm not a 'poor child,' Uncle Dick," expostulated the Imp; "I'm a gallant knight and——"

"—The blame of my fault, Lisbeth," I continued, "I alone must face your just resentment, for——"

"Hush!" she whispered, glancing hastily about.

"—For, by means of a ladder, Lisbeth, a common or garden ladder——"

"Oh, do be quiet!" she said, and laid her hand upon my lips, which I immediately imprisoned there, but for a moment only; the next it was snatched away as there came the unmistakable sound of some one approaching.

"Come along, Auntie Lisbeth," whispered the Imp; "fear not, we'll rescue you."

Oh! surely there was magic in the air to-night; for, with a swift, dexterous movement, Lisbeth had swept her long train across her arm, and we were running hand in hand, all three of us, running across lawns and down winding paths between yew hedges, sometimes so close together that I could feel a tress of her fragrant hair brushing my face with a touch almost like a caress. Surely, surely, there was magic in the air to-night!

Suddenly Lisbeth stopped, flushed and panting.

"Well!" she exclaimed, staring from

me to the Imp, and back again, "was ever anything so mad!"

"Everything is mad to-night," I said; "it's the moon!"

"To think of my running away like this with two—two———"

"Interlopers," I suggested.

"I really ought to be very, very angry with you—both of you, she said, trying to frown.

"No, don't be angry with us, Auntie Lisbeth," pleaded the Imp, " 'cause you are a lovely lady in a castle grim, an' we are two gallant knights, so we had to come an' rescue you; an' you never came to kiss me good-night, an' I'm awfull' sorry 'bout painting Dorothy's face—really!"

"Imp," cried Lisbeth, falling on her knees regardless of her silks and laces, "Imp, come and kiss me." The Imp drew out a decidedly grubby handkerchief, and, having rubbed his lips with it, obeyed.

"Now, Uncle Dick!" he said, and offered me the grubby handkerchief. Lisbeth actually blushed.

"Reginald!" she exclaimed, "whatever put such an idea into your head?"

"Oh! everybody's always kissing somebody you know," he nodded; "an' it's Uncle Dick's turn now."

Lisbeth rose from her knees and began to pat her rebellious hair into order. Now, as she raised her arms, her shawl very naturally slipped to the ground; and standing there, with her eyes laughing up at me beneath their dark lashes, with the moonlight in her hair, and gleaming upon the snow of her neck and shoulders, she had never seemed quite so bewilderingly, temptingly beautiful before.

"Dick," she said, "I must go back at once—before they miss me."

"Go back!" I repeated, "never—that is, not yet."

"But suppose any one saw us!" she said, with a hairpin in her mouth.

"They shan't," I answered; "you will see to that, won't you, Imp?"

" 'Course I will, Uncle Dick!"

"Then go you, Sir Knight, and keep faithful ward behind yon apple tree, and let no base varlet hither come; that is, if you see any one, be sure to tell me." The Imp saluted and promptly disappeared behind the apple tree in question, while I stood watching Lisbeth's dexterous fingers and striving to remember a line from Keats descriptive of a beautiful woman in the moonlight. Before I could call it to mind, however, Lisbeth interrupted me.

"Don't you think you might pick up my shawl instead of staring at me as if I was——"

"The most beautiful woman in the world!" I put in.

—"Who is catching her death of

cold," she laughed, yet for all her light tone her eyes drooped before mine as I obediently wrapped the shawl about her, in the doing of which, my arm being round her, very naturally stayed there, and— wonder of wonders, was not repulsed. And at this very moment, from the shadowy trees behind us, came the rich, clear song of a nightingale.

Oh! most certainly the air was full of magic to-night!

"Dick," said Lisbeth very softly as the trilling notes died away, "I thought one could only dream such a night as this is."

"And yet life might hold many such for you and me, if you would only let it, Lisbeth," I reminded her. She did not answer.

"Not far from the village of Down, in Kent," I began.

"There stands a house," she put in,

staring up at the moon with dreamy eyes.

"Yes."

"A very old house, with twisted Tudor chimneys and pointed gables— you see I have it all by heart, Dick— a house with wide stairways and long pannelled chambers———"

"Very empty and desolate at present," I added. "And amongst other things, there is a rose-garden—they call it My Lady's Garden, Lisbeth, though no lady has trod its winding paths for years and years. But I have dreamed, many and many a time, that we stood among the roses, she and I, upon just such another night as this is. So I keep the old house ready and the gardens freshly trimmed, ready for my lady's coming; must I wait much longer, Lisbeth?" As I ended the nightingale took up the story, pleading my cause for me, filling the air with a melody now appealing, now commanding, until it gradually died away in one long note of passionate entreaty.

Lisbeth sighed and turned towards me, but as she did so I felt a tug at my coat, and, looking round, beheld the Imp.

"Uncle Dick," he said, his eyes studiously averted, doubtless on account of the position of my arm, "here's Mr. Selwyn!"

With a sudden exclamation Lisbeth started from me and gathered up her skirts to run.

"Whereaway, my Imp?"

"Coming across the lawn."

"Reginald," I said, solemnly, listen to me; you must sally out upon him with lance in rest, tell him you are a Knight-errant, wishful to uphold the glory of that faire ladye, your Auntie Lisbeth, and whatever happens you must manage to keep him away from here, do you understand?"

"Yes, only I do wish I'd brought my trusty sword, you know," he sighed.

"Never mind that now, Imp."

"Will Auntie Lisbeth be quite——"

"She will be all right."

"I suppose if you put your arm ——"

"Never mind my arm, Imp, go!"

"Then fare thee well!" said he, and with a melodramatic flourish of his lance, trotted off.

"What did he mean about your arm, Dick?"

"Probably this!" I answered, slipping it around her again.

"But you must get away at once," whispered Lisbeth; "if Mr. Selwyn should see you——"

"I intend that he shall. Oh, it will be quite simple; while he is talking to me you can get back to the——"

"Hush!" she whispered, laying her fingers on my lips; "listen!"

"Hallo, Mr. Selwyn!" came in the Imp's familiar tones.

"Why, good Heavens!" exclaimed another voice, much too near to be pleasant, "what on earth are you doing here—and at this time of night?"

"Looking for base varlets!"

"Don't you know that all little boys —all nice little boys—should have been in bed hours ago?"

"But I'm not a nice little boy; I'm a Knight-errant; would you like to get a lance, Mr. Selwyn, an' break it with me to the glory of my Auntie Lisbeth?"

"The question is, what has become of her?" said Mr. Selwyn. We waited almost breathlessly for the answer.

"Oh! I 'specks she's somewhere looking at the moon; everybody looks at the moon, you know; Betty does, an' the lady with the man with a funny name 'bout being bald, an'——"

"I think you had better come up to the house," said Mr. Selwyn.

"Do you think you could get me an ice cream if I did?" asked the Imp, persuasively; "nice an' pink, you know, with——"

"An ice!" repeated Mr. Selwyn; "I wonder how many you have had already to-night?"

The time for action was come.

"Lisbeth," I said, "we must go; such happiness as this could not last; how should it? I think it is given us to dream over in less happy days. For me it will be a memory to treasure always, and yet there might be one thing more—a little thing, Lisbeth—can you guess?" She did not speak, but I saw the dimple come and go at the corner of her mouth, so I stooped and kissed her. For a moment, all too brief, we stood thus, with the glory of the moonlight about us; then

I was hurrying across the lawn after Selwyn and the Imp.

"Ah, Mr. Selwyn!" I said as I overtook them, "so you have found him, have you?" Mr. Selwyn turned to regard me, surprise writ large upon him, from the points of his immaculate, patent-leather shoes, to the parting of his no less immaculate hair.

"So very good of you," I continued; "you see he is such a difficult object to recover when once he gets mislaid; really, I'm awfully obliged." Mr. Selwyn's attitude was politely formal. He bowed.

"What is it to-night," he inquired, "pirates"?

"Hardly so bad as that," I returned; "to-night the air is full of the clash of armour and the ring of steel; if you do not hear it that is not our fault."

"An' the woods are full of caddish barons and caitiff knaves, you know, aren't they, Uncle Dick?"

MY LADY CAPRICE

"Certainly," I nodded, with lance
and spear-point twinkling through the
gloom; but in the silver glory of the
moon, Mr. Selwyn, walk errant damo-
zels and ladyes faire, and again, if
you don't see them, the loss is yours."
As I spoke, away upon the terrace a
grey shadow paused a moment ere it
was swallowed in the brilliance of the
ball-room; seeing which I did not
mind the slightly superior smile that
curved Mr. Selwyn's very precise
moustache; after all, my rhapsody
had not been altogether thrown away.

As I ended, the opening bars of a
waltz floated out to us. Mr. Selwyn
glanced back over his shoulder.

"Ah! I suppose you can find your
way out?" he inquired.

"Oh, yes, thanks."

"Then if you will excuse me, I think
I'll leave you to—ah—to do it; the
next dance is beginning, and—ah
____"

"Certainly," I said, "of course—good-night, and much obliged—really!" Mr. Selwyn bowed, and, turning away, left us to our own resources.

"I should have liked another ice, Uncle Dick," sighed the Imp, regretfully.

"Knights never ate ice cream!" I said, as we set off along the nearest path.

"Uncle Dick," said the Imp suddenly, "do you 'spose Mr. Selwyn wants to put his arm round Auntie Lis——"

"Possibly!"

"An' do you 'spose that Auntie Lisbeth wants Mr. Selwyn to——"

"I don't know—of course not—er —kindly shut up, will you, Imp?"

"I only wanted to know, you know," he murmured.

Therewith we walked on in silence and I fell to dreaming of Lisbeth

again, of how she had sighed, of the
look in her eyes as she turned to me
with her answer trembling on her lips
—the answer which the Imp had inad-
vertently cut short.

In this frame of mind I drew near
to that corner of the garden where
she had stood with me, that quiet,
shady corner, which henceforth would
remain enshrined within my memory
for her sake, which——

I stopped suddenly short at the sight
of two figures—one in the cap and
apron of a waiting maid and the other
in the gorgeous plush and gold braid
of a footman; and they were standing
upon the very spot where Lisbeth and
I had stood, and in almost the exact
attitude—it was desecration.

I stood stock still despite the Imp's
frantic tugs at my coat, all other feelings swallowed up in one of half-
amused resentment. Thus the resplendent footman happened to turn

his head, presently espied me, and removing his plush-clad arm from the waist of the trim maid-servant, and doubling his fists, strode towards us with a truly terrible mien.

"And w'ot might your game be?" he inquired, with that supercilious air inseparable to plush and gold braid; "oh, I know your kind, I do—I know yer!"

"Then, fellow," quoth I, "I know not thee, by Thor, I swear it and Og the Terrible, King of Bashan!"

" 'Ogs is it?" said he indignantly, "don't get trying to come over me with yer 'ogs; no nor yet yer fellers! The question is, wo't are you 'anging round 'ere for?" Now, possibly deceived by my pacific attitude, or inspired by the bright eyes of the trim maid-servant, he seized me, none too gently, by the collar, to the horrified dismay of the Imp.

"Nay, but I will give thee moneys
_____"

"You are a-going to come up to the
'ouse with me, and no blooming non-
sense, either; d'ye 'ear?"

"Then must I needs smite thee for a
barbarous dog—hence—base slave—
begone!" Wherewith I delivered
what is technically known in "sport-
ing" circles as a "right hook to the
ear," followed by a "left swing to the
chin," and my assailant immediately
disappeared behind a bush, with a
flash of pink silk calves and buckled
shoes. Then, while the trim maid-
servant filled the air with her lamen-
tations, the Imp and I ran hot-foot
for the wall, over which I bundled
him neck and crop, and we set off pell-
mell along the river-path.

"Oh, Uncle Dick," he panted, "how
—how fine you are! you knocked yon
footman—I mean varlet—from his
saddle like—like anything. Oh, I do

wish you would play like this every night!"

"Heaven forbid!" I exclaimed fervently.

Coming at last to the shrubbery gate, we paused awhile to regain our breath.

"Uncle Dick," said the Imp, regarding me with a thoughtful eye, "did you see his arm—I mean before you smote him 'hip and thigh'?"

"I did."

"It was round her waist."

"Imp, it was."

"Just like Peter's?"

"Yes."

"An' the man with the funny name?"

"Archibald's, yes."

"An'—an'——"

"And mine," I put in, seeing he paused.

"Uncle Dick—why?"

"Ah! who knows, Imp—perhaps it

was the Moon-magic. And now by my troth! 'tis full time all good knights were snoring, so hey for bed and the Slumber-world!"

The ladder was dragged from its hiding place, and the Imp, having mounted, watched me from his window as I returned it to the laurels for very obvious reasons.

"We didn't see any fairies, did we, Uncle Dick?"

"Well, I think I did, Imp, just for a moment; I may have been mistaken, of course, but anyhow, it has been a very wonderful night all the same. And so—God rest you, fair Knight!"

V

THE sun blazed down, as any truly self-respecting sun should, on a fine August afternoon; yet its heat was tempered by a soft, cool breeze that just stirred the leaves above my head.

The river was busy whispering many things to the reeds, things which, had I been wise enough to understand, might have helped me to write many wonderful books, for, as it is so very old, and has both seen and heard so much, it is naturally very wise. But alas! being ignorant of the language of rivers, I had to content myself with my own dreams, and the large, speckled frog, that sat beside me, watching the flow of the river with his big, gold-rimmed eyes.

He was happy enough I was sure.
There was a complacent satisfaction
in every line of his fat, mottled body.
And as I watched him my mind very
naturally reverted to the "Pickwick
Papers," and I repeated Mrs. Lyon-
Hunter's deathless ode, beginning:

> Can I see thee panting, dying,
> On a log,
> Expiring frog!

The big, green frog beside me list-
ened with polite attention, but, on the
whole, seemed strangely unmoved.
Remembering the book in my pocket,
I took it out; an old book, with battered leathern covers, which has
passed through many hands since it
was first published, more than two
hundred years ago.

Indeed it is a wonderful, a most delightful book, known to the world as
"The Compleat Angler," in which, to
be sure, one may read something of

fish and fishing, but more about old Izaac's lovable self, his sunny streams and shady pools, his buxom milkmaids, and sequestered inns, and his kindly animadversions upon men and things in general. Yet, as I say, he does occasionally speak of fish and fishing, and amongst other matters, concerning live frogs as bait, after describing the properest method of impaling one upon the hook, he ends with this injunction:

Treat it as though you loved it, that it may live the longer!

Up till now the frog had preserved his polite attentiveness in a manner highly creditable to his upbringing, but this proved too much; his overcharged feelings burst from him in a hoarse croak, and he disappeared into the river with a splash.

"Good-afternoon, Uncle Dick!" said a voice at my elbow, and looking round, I beheld Dorothy. Beneath one arm she carried the fluffy kitten, and in the other hand a scrap of paper.

"I promised Reginald to give you this," she continued, "and—oh yes— I was to say 'Hist!' first."

"Really! And why were you to say 'Hist'?"

"Oh, because all Indians always say 'Hist!' you know."

"To be sure they do," I answered; "but am I to understand that you are an Indian?"

"Not to-day," replied Dorothy, shaking her head. "Last time Reginald painted me Auntie was awfull' angry —it took her and nurse ages to get it all off—the war-paint, I mean—so I'm afraid I can't be an Indian again!"

"That's very unfortunate!" I said.

"Yes, isn't it; but nobody can be an

Indian chief without any war-paint, can they?"

"Certainly not," I answered. "You seem to know a great deal about it."

"Oh, yes," nodded Dorothy. "Reginald has a book all about Indians and full of pictures—and here's the letter," she ended, and slipped it into my hand.

Smoothing out its many folds and creases, I read aloud, as follows:

To my pail-face brother:

Ere another moon, Spotted Snaik will be upon the war-path, and red goar shall flo in buckkit-fulls.

"It sounds dreadful, doesn't it?" said Dorothy, hugging her kitten.

"Horrible!" I returned.

"He got it out of the book, you know," she went on, "but I put in the part about the buckets—a bucket holds such an awful lot, don't you think? But there's some more on the other page." Obediently I turned, and read:

'ere another moon, scalps shall dangel at belt of Spotted Snaik, for in his futsteps lurk deth, and distruksion. But fear not pail-face, thou art my brother—fairwell.

Sined

SPOTTED SNAIK.

"There was lots more, but we couldn't get it in," said Dorothy. Squeezed up into a corner I found this postscript:

If you will come and be an Indian Cheef unkel dick, I will make you a spear, and you can be Blood-in-the-Eye. He was a fine chap and nobody could beat him except Spotted Snaik, will you Unkel dick?

"He wants you to write an answer, and I'm to take it to him," said Dorothy.

"Blood-in-the-Eye!" I repeated; "no, I'm afraid not. I shouldn't object so much to becoming a red-skin—for a time—but Blood-in-the-Eye! Really, Dorothy, I'm afraid I couldn't manage that."

"He was very brave," returned Dorothy, "and awfull' strong, and could —could 'throw his lance with such unerring aim, as to pin his foe to the nearest tree—in the twinkle of an eye.' That's in the book, you know."

"There certainly must be a great deal of satisfaction in pinning one's foe to a tree," I nodded.

"Y-e-e-s, I suppose so," said Dorothy rather dubiously.

"And where is Spotted Snake—I mean, what is he doing?"

"Oh, he's down by the river with his bow and arrow, scouting for canoes. It was great fun! He shot at a man in a boat—and nearly hit him, and the man got very angry indeed, so we had to hide among the bushes, just like real Indians. Oh, it was fine!"

"But your Auntie Lisbeth said you weren't to play near the river, you know," I said.

"That's what I told him," returned Dorothy, "but he said that Indians didn't have any aunts, and then I didn't know what to say. What do you think about it, Uncle Dick?"

"Well," I answered, "now I come to consider, I can't remember ever having heard of an Indian's aunt."

"Poor things!" said Dorothy, giving the fluffy kitten a kiss between the ears.

"Yes, it's hard on them, perhaps, and yet," I added thoughtfully, "an aunt is sometimes rather a mixed blessing. Still, whether an Indian possesses an aunt or not, the fact remains that water has an unpleasant habit of wetting one, and on the whole, I think I'll go and see what Spotted Snake is up to."

"Then I think I'll come with you a

MY LADY CAPRICE

little way," said Dorothy, as I rose.
"You see, I have to get Louise her
afternoon's milk."

"And how is Louise?" I inquired,
pulling the fluffy kitten's nearest ear.

"Very well, thank you," answered
Dorothy demurely; "but oh dear me!
kittens 'are such a constant source of
worry and anxiety!' Auntie Lisbeth
sometimes says that about Reginald
and me. I wonder what she would
say if we were kittens!"

"Bye the bye, where is your Auntie
Lisbeth?" I asked in a strictly conversational tone.

"Well, she's lying in the old boat."

"In the old boat!" I repeated.

"Yes," nodded Dorothy; "when it's
nice and warm and sleepy, like to-day,
she takes a book, and a pillow, and a
sunshade, and she goes and lies in the
old boat under the Water-stairs.
There, just look at this naughty
Louise!" she broke off, as the kitten

scrambled up to her shoulder and stood there, balancing itself very dextrously with curious angular movements of its tail; "that's because she thinks I've forgotten her milk, you know; she's dreadfully impatient, but I suppose I must humour her this once. Good-afternoon!" And, having given me her hand in her demure, old-fashioned way, Dorothy hurried off, the kitten still perched upon her shoulder, its tail jerking spasmodically with her every step.

In a little while I came in view of the Water-stairs, yet although I paused more than once to look about me, I saw no sign of the Imp. Thinking he was most probably 'in ambush' somewhere, I continued my way, whistling an air out of "The Geisha" to attract his notice. Ten minutes or more elapsed, however, without any sign of him, and I was already close to the stairs, when I stopped whistling all at once, and holding my breath, crept forward on tiptoe.

There before me was the old boat, and in it—her cheek upon a crimson cushion and the sun making a glory of her tumbled hair—was Lisbeth—asleep.

Being come as near as I dared for fear of waking her, I sat down, and lighting my pipe, fell to watching her—the up-curving shadow of her lashes, the gleam of teeth between the scarlet of her parted lips, and the soft undulation of her bosom. And from the heavy braids of her hair my glance wandered down to the little tan shoe peeping at me beneath her skirt, and I called to mind how Goethe has said:

'A pretty foot is not only a continual joy, but it is the one element of beauty that defies the assaults of Time.'

Sometimes a butterfly hovered past,

a bee filled the air with his drone, or
a bird settled for a moment upon the
stairs near-by to preen a ruffled
feather, while soft and drowsy with
distance came the ceaseless roar of the
weir.

I do not know how long I had sat
thus, supremely content, when I was
suddenly aroused by a rustling close
at hand.

"Hist!"

I looked up sharply, and beheld
a head, a head adorned with sundry feathers, and a face hid-
eously streaked with red and green
paint; but there was no mistak-
ing those golden curls—it was the
Imp!

"Hist!" he repeated, bringing out
the word with a prolonged hiss, and
then—before I could even guess at
his intention—there was the swift
gleam of a knife, a splash of the severed painter, and caught by the tide

the old boat swung out, and was adrift.

The Imp stood gazing on his handiwork with wide eyes, and then as I leaped to my feet something in my look seemed to frighten him, for without a word he turned and fled.

But all my attention was centred in the boat, which was drifting slowly into mid-stream with Lisbeth still fast asleep. And as I watched its sluggish progress, with a sudden chill I remembered the weir, which foamed and roared only a short half-mile away. If the boat once got drawn into that——!

Now, I am quite aware that under these circumstances the right and proper thing for me to have done, would have been to throw aside my coat, tear off my boots, etc., and "boldly breast the foamy flood." But I did neither, for the simple reason that once within the 'foamy flood'

aforesaid, there would have been very
little chance of my ever getting out
again, for—let me confess the fact
with the blush of shame—I am no
swimmer.

Yet I was not idle, far otherwise.
Having judged the distance between
the drifting boat and the bank, I began running along, seeking the thing
I wanted. And presently, sure
enough, I found it—a great pollard
oak, growing upon the edge of the
water, that identical tree with the
'stickie-out' branches which has already figured in these narratives as the
hiding-place of a certain pair of silk
stockings.

Hastily swinging myself up, I got
astride the lowest branch, which pro-
jected out over the water. I had dis-
tanced the boat by some hundred
yards, and as I sat there I watched
its drift, one minute full of hope, and
the next as miserably uncertain.

My obvious intention was to crawl out upon the branch until it bent with my weight, and so let myself into, or as near the boat as possible.

It was close now, so close that I could see the gleam of Lisbeth's hair and the point of the little tan shoe. With my eyes on this, I writhed my way along the bough, which bent more and more as I neared the end. Here I hung, swaying up and down and to and fro in a highly unpleasant manner, while I waited the crucial moment.

Never upon this whole round earth did anything creep as that boat did. There was a majestic deliberation in its progress that positively maddened me. I remember to have once read an article somewhere upon the "Sensibility of Material Things," or something of the sort, which I had forgotten long since, but as I hung there suspended between heaven and earth, it came back to

me with a rush, and I was perfectly
certain that, recognising my precari-
ous position, that time-worn, ancient
boat checked its speed out of "pure
cussedness."

But all things have an end, and so,
little by little the blunt bow crept
nearer until it was in the very shade
of my tree. Grasping the branch, I
let myself swing at arm's length; and
then I found that I was at least a
foot too near the bank. Edging my
way, therefore, still further along the
branch, I kicked out in a desperate en-
deavour to reach the boat, and, the
bough swaying with me, caught my
toe inside the gunwale, drew it under
me, and loosing my grasp, was sprawl-
ing upon my hands and knees, but safe
aboard.

To pick myself up was the work of
a moment, yet scarcely had I done so,
when Lisbeth opened her eyes, and
sitting up, stared about her.

"Why—where am I?" she exclaimed.

"On the river," I answered cheerfully. "Glorious afternoon, Lisbeth, isn't it?"

"How—in—the—world did you get here?" she inquired.

"Well," I answered, "I might say I dropped in as it were." Lisbeth brushed the hair from her temples, and turned to me with an imperious gesture.

"Then please take me back at once," she said.

"I would with pleasure," I returned, "only that you forgot to bring the oars."

"Why, then, we are adrift!" she said, staring at me with frightened eyes, and clasping her hands nervously.

"We are," I nodded; "but, then, it's perfect weather for boating, Lisbeth!" And I began to look about for some-

thing that might serve as a paddle.
But the stretchers had disappeared
long since—the old tub was a sheer
hulk, so to speak. An attempt to tear
up a floor board resulted only in a
broken nail and bleeding fingers; so
I presently desisted, and rolling up my
sleeves endeavoured to paddle with my
hands. But finding this equally futile,
I resumed my coat, and took out pipe
and tobacco.

"Oh, Dick! is there nothing you can
do?" she asked, with a brave attempt
to steady the quiver in her voice.

"With your permission, I'll smoke,
Lisbeth."

"But the weir!" she cried; "have you
forgotten the weir?"

"No," I answered, shaking my head;
"it has a way of obtruding itself on
one's notice——"

"Oh, it sounds hateful—hateful!"
she said with a shiver.

"Like a strong wind among trees!"

I nodded, as I filled my pipe. We were approaching a part of the river where it makes a sharp bend to the right; and well I knew what lay beyond—the row of posts, painted white, with the foam and bubble of seething water below. We should round that bend in about ten minutes, I judged; long before then we might see a boat, to be sure; if not—well, if the worst happened, I could but do my best; in the meantime I would smoke a pipe; but I will admit my fingers trembled as I struck a match.

"It sounds horribly close!" said Lisbeth.

"Sound is very deceptive, you know," I answered.

"Only last month a boat went over, and the man was drowned!" shuddered Lisbeth.

"Poor chap!" I said. "Of course it's different at night—the river is aw-

fully deserted then, you know, and
_____"

"But it happened in broad daylight!" said Lisbeth, almost in a whisper. She was sitting half turned from me, her gaze fixed on the bend of the river, and by chance her restless hand had found and begun to fumble with the severed painter.

So we drifted on, watching the gliding banks, while every moment the roar of the weir grew louder and more threatening.

"Dick," she said suddenly, "we can never pass that awful place without oars!" and she began to tie knots in the rope with fingers that shook pitifully.

"Oh, I don't know!" I returned, with an assumption of ease I was very far from feeling; "and then, of course, we are bound to meet a boat or something——"

"But suppose we don't?"

"Oh, well, we aren't there yet—and er—let's talk of fish."

"Ah, Dick," she cried, "how can you treat the matter so lightly when we may be tossing down there in that awful water so very soon! We can never pass that weir without oars, and you know it, and—and—oh, Dick, why did you do it—how could you have been so mad?"

"Do what?" I inquired, staring.

With a sudden gesture she rose to her knees and fronted me.

"This!" she cried, and held up the severed painter. "It has been cut! Oh, Dick! Dick! how could you be so mad."

"Lisbeth!" I exclaimed, "do you mean to say that you think——"

"I know!" she broke in, and turning away, hid her face in her hands.

We were not so very far from the bend now, and seeing this, a sudden inspiration came upon me, by means

of which I might prove her mind towards me once and for all; and as
she kneeled before me with averted
face, I leaned forward and took her
hands in mine.

"Lisbeth," I said, "supposing I did
cut the boat adrift, like a—a fool—
endangering your life for a mad,
thoughtless whim—could you forgive
me?"

For a long moment she remained
without answering, then very slowly
she raised her head:

"Oh, Dick!" was all she said, but
in her eyes I read the wonder of wonders.

"But, Lisbeth," I stammered, "could
you still love me—even—even if,
through my folly, the worst should
happen and we—we——"

"I don't think I shall be so very
much afraid, Dick, if you will hold
me close like this," she whispered.

The voice of the weir had swelled

into a roar by now, yet I paid little heed; for me, all fear was swallowed up in a great wondering happiness.

"Dick," she whispered, "you will hold me tight, you will not let me go when—when——"

"Never," I answered; "nothing could ever take you from me now." As I spoke I raised my eyes, and glancing about beheld something which altered the whole aspect of affairs—something which changed tragedy into comedy all in a moment—a boat was coming slowly round the bend.

"Lisbeth, look up!" With a sigh she obeyed, her clasp tightening on mine, and a dreadful expectation in her eyes. Then all at once it was gone, her pale cheeks grew suddenly scarlet, and she slipped from my arms; and thereafter I noticed how very carefully her eyes avoided mine.

The boat came slowly into view, im-

pelled by one who rowed with exactly
that amount of splashing which speaks
the true-born Cockney. By dint of
much exertion and more splashing, he
presently ranged alongside in answer
to my hail.

"Wo't—a haccident then?" he inquired.

"Something of the sort," I nodded.
"Will you be so kind as to tow us to
the bank yonder?"

"Hanythink to hoblige!" he grinned,
and having made fast the painter,
proceeded to splash us to terra-firma.
Which done, he grinned again, waved
his hat, and splashed upon his way. I
made the boat secure and turned to
Lisbeth. She was staring away towards the weir.

"Lisbeth," I began.

"I thought just now that—that it
was the end!" she said, and shiv-
ered.

"And at such times," I added, "one

sometimes says things one would not have said under ordinary circumstances. My dear, I quite understand—quite, and I'll try to forget— you needn't fear."

"Do you think you can?" she asked, turning to look at me.

"I can but try," I answered. Now as I spoke I wasn't sure, but I thought I saw the pale ghost of the dimple by her mouth.

We walked back side by side along the river-path, very silently, for the most part, yet more than once I caught her regarding me covertly and with a puzzled air.

"Well?" I said at last, tentatively.

"I was wondering why you did it, Dick? Oh, it was mean! cruel! wicked! How could you?"

"Oh, well"—and I shrugged my shoulders, anathematising the Imp mentally the while.

"If I hadn't noticed that the rope

was freshly cut, I should have thought
it an accident," she went on.

"Naturally!" I said.

"And then, again, how came you in
the boat?"

"To be sure!" I nodded.

"Still, I can scarcely believe that you
would wilfully jeopardise both our
lives—my life!"

"A man who would do such a thing,"
I exclaimed, carried away by the heat
of the moment, "would be a—a———"

"Yes," said Lisbeth quickly, "he
would."

"—And utterly beyond the pale of
all forgiveness!"

"Yes," said Lisbeth, "of course."

"And," I was beginning again, but
meeting her searching glance, stopped.
"And you forgave me, Lisbeth," I
ended.

"Did I?" she said, with raised
brows.

"Didn't you?"

"Not that I remember."

"In the boat?"

"I never *said* so."

"Not in words, perhaps, but you implied as much." Lisbeth had the grace to blush.

"Do I understand that I am not forgiven after all?"

"Not until I know why you did such a mad, thoughtless trick," she answered, with that determined set of her chin which I knew so well.

That I should thus shoulder the responsibility for the Imp's misdeeds was ridiculous, and wrong as it was unjust, for if ever boy deserved punishment that boy was the Imp. And yet, probably because he was the Imp, or because of that school-boy honour which forbids "sneaking," and which I carried with me still, I held my peace; seeing which, Lisbeth turned and left me.

I stood where I was, with head bent

in an attitude suggestive of innocence, broken hopes, and gentle resignation, but in vain; she never once looked back. Still, martyr though I was, the knowledge that I had immolated myself upon the altar of friendship filled me with a sense of conscious virtue that I found not ill-pleasing. Howbeit, seeing I am but human after all, I sat down and re-filling my pipe, fell once more anathematising the Imp.

"Hist!"

A small shape flittered from behind an adjacent tree, and lo! the subject of my thoughts stood before me.

"Imp," I said, "come here." He obeyed readily. "When you cut that rope and set your Auntie Lisbeth adrift, you didn't remember the man who was drowned in the weir last month, did you?"

"No!" he answered, staring.

"Of course not," I nodded; "but all the same it is not your fault that your

Auntie Lisbeth is not drowned—just as he was."

"Oh!" exclaimed the Imp, and his beloved bow slipped from his nerveless fingers.

"Imp," I went on, "it was a wicked thing to cut that rope, a mean, cruel trick. Don't you think so?"

"I 'specks it was, Uncle Dick."

"Don't you think you ought to be punished?" He nodded. "Very well," I answered, "I'll punish you myself. Go and cut me a nice, straight switch," and I handed him my open penknife. Round-eyed, the Imp obeyed, and for a space there was a prodigious cracking and snapping of sticks. In a little while he returned with three, also the blade of my knife was broken, for which he was profusely apologetic.

"Now," I said, as I selected the weapon fittest for the purpose, "I am going to strike you hard on either hand with this stick—that is, if you think you deserve it."

"Was Auntie Lisbeth nearly drowned —really?" he inquired.

"Very nearly, and was only saved by a chance."

"All right, Uncle Dick, hit me," he said, and held out his hand. The stick whizzed and fell—once—twice. I saw his face grow scarlet and the tears leap to his eyes, but he uttered no sound.

"Did it hurt very much, my Imp?" I inquired, as I tossed the stick aside.

He nodded, not trusting himself to speak, while I turned to light my pipe, wasting three matches quite fruitlessly.

"Uncle Dick," he burst out at last, struggling manfully against his sobs, "I—I'm awfull'—sorry——"

"Oh, it's all right now, Imp. Shake hands!" Joyfully the little, grimy fingers clasped mine, and from that moment I think there grew up between us a new understanding.

"Why, Imp, my darling, you're crying!" exclaimed a voice, and with a rustle of skirts Lisbeth was down before him on her knees.

"I know I am—'cause I'm awfull' sorry—an' Uncle Dick's whipped my hands—an' I'm glad!"

"Whipped your hands!" cried Lisbeth, clasping him closer, and glaring at me, "whipped your hands—how dare he! What for?"

"'Cause I cut the rope an' let the boat go away with you, an' you might have been drowned dead in the weir, an' I'm awfull' glad Uncle Dick whipped me."

"O-h-h!" exclaimed Lisbeth, and it was a very long-drawn "oh!" indeed.

"I don't know what made me do it," continued the Imp. "I 'specks it was my new knife—it was so nice an' sharp, you know."

"Well, it's all right now, my Imp,"
I said, fumbling for a match in a
singularly clumsy manner. "If you
ask me, I think we are all better
friends than ever—or should be. I
know I should be fonder of your
Auntie Lisbeth even than before, and
take greater care of her, if I were you.
And—and now take her in to tea, my
Imp, and—and see that she has plenty
to eat," and lifting my hat I turned
away. But Lisbeth was beside me,
and her hand was on my arm before I
had gone a yard.

"We are having tea in the same old
place—under the trees. If you would
care to—to—would you?"

"Yes, do—oh do, Uncle Dick!"
cried the Imp. "I'll go and tell Jane to
set a place for you," and he bounded
off.

"I didn't hit him very hard," I said,
breaking a somewhat awkward silence;
"but you see there are some things a

gentleman cannot do. I think he understands now."

"Oh, Dick!" she said very softly; "and to think I could imagine you had done such a thing—you; and to think that you should let me think you had done such a thing—and all to shield that Imp? Oh, Dick! no wonder he is so fond of you. He never talks of any one but you—I grow quite jealous sometimes. But, Dick, how *did* you get into that boat?"

"By means of a tree with 'stickie-out' branches."

"Do you mean to say——"

"That, as I told you before, I dropped in, as it were."

"But supposing you had slipped?"

"But I didn't."

"And you can't swim a stroke!"

"Not that I know of."

"Oh, Dick! can you ever forgive me?"

"On three conditions."

"Well?"

"First, that you let me remember everything you said to me while we were drifting down to the weir."

"That depends, Dick. And the second?"

"The second lies in the fact that not far from the village of Down, in Kent, there stands an old house—a quaint old place that is badly in want of some one to live in it—an old house that is lonely for a woman's sweet presence and gentle, busy hands, Lisbeth!"

"And the third?" she asked very softly.

"Surely you can guess that?"

"No, I can't, and, besides, there's Dorothy coming—and—oh, Dick!"

"Why, Auntie," exclaimed Dorothy, as she came up, "how red you are! I knew you'd get sunburned, lying in that old boat without a parasol! But, then, she will do it, Uncle Dick—oh, she will do it!"

VI

THE OUTLAW

EVERYBODY knew old Jasper Trent, the Crimean Veteran who had helped to beat the "Roosians and the Proosians," and who, so it was rumored, had more wounds upon his worn, bent body than there were months in the year.

The whole village was proud of old Jasper, proud of his age, proud of his wounds, and proud of the medals that shone resplendent upon his shrunken breast.

Any day he might have been seen hobbling along by the river, or pottering among the flowers in his little garden, but oftener still sitting on the bench in the sunshine beside the door of the "Three Jolly Anglers."

Indeed, they made a fitting pair, the worn old soldier and the ancient inn, alike both long behind the times, dreaming of the past, rather than the future; which seemed to me like an invisible bond between them. Thus, when old Jasper fell ill and taking to his bed had it moved opposite the window where he could lie with his eyes upon the battered gables of the inn—I for one could understand the reason.

The Three Jolly Anglers is indeed ancient, its early records long since lost beneath the dust of centuries; yet the years have but served to mellow it. Men have lived and died, nations have waxed and waned, still it stands, all unchanged beside the river, watching the Great Tragedy which we call "Life" with that same look of supreme wisdom, that half-waggish, half-kindly air, which I have already mentioned once before.

MY LADY CAPRICE

I think such inns as this must extend some subtle influence upon those who meet regularly within their walls—these Sons of the Soil, horny-handed, and for the most part grey of head and bent with over much following of the plough. Quiet of voice are they, and profoundly sedate of gesture, while upon their wrinkled brows there sits that spirit of calm content which it is given so few of us to know.

Chief among these, and held in much respect, was old Jasper Trent. Within their circle he had been wont to sit ensconced in his elbow-chair beside the hearth, his by long use and custom, and not to be usurped; and while the smoke rose slowly from their pipe-bowls, and the ale foamed in tankards at their elbows, he would recount some tale of battle and sudden death —now in the freezing trenches before Sebastopol, now upon the blood-stained heights of Inkermann. Yet,

and I noticed it was always towards
the end of his second tankard, the old
man would lose the thread of his
story, whatever it might be, and take
up the topic of "The Bye Jarge."

I was at first naturally perplexed as
to whom he could mean, until Mr.
Amos Baggett, the landlord, informed
me on the quiet that the "bye Jarge"
was none other than old Jasper's only
son—a man now some forty years of
age—who, though promising well in
his youth, had "gone wrong"—and
was at that moment serving a long
term of imprisonment for burglary;
further, that upon the day of his son's
conviction old Jasper had had a
"stroke," and was never quite the
same after, all recollection of the
event being completely blotted from
his mind, so that he persisted in thinking and speaking of his son as still a
boy.

"That bye were a wonder!" he

would say, looking round with a kindling eye; "went away to make 'is fortun' 'e did—oh! 'e were a gen'us were that bye Jarge! You, Amos Baggett, were 'e a gen'us or were 'e not?"

" 'E were!" Mr. Baggett would answer, with a slow nod.

"Look'ee, sir, do'ee see that theer clock?"—and he would point with a bony, tremulous finger—"stopped it were—got sum'mat wrong wi' its inn'ards—wouldn't stir a finger—dead it were! But that bye Jarge 'e see it 'e did—give it a look over 'e did, an' wi' nout but 'is two 'ands set it a-goin' good as ever! You, Silas Madden, you remember as 'e done it wi' 'is two 'ands?"

" 'Is two 'ands!" Silas would repeat solemnly.

"An' it's gone ever since!" old Jasper would croak triumphantly. "Oh! 'e were a gen'us were my bye Jarge. 'E'll come a-marchin' back to 'is old

feyther, some day, wi' 'is pockets
stuffed full o' money an' banki-notes
—I knaw—I knaw, old Jasper bean't
a fule."

And herewith, lifting up his old,
cracked voice, he would strike up
"The British Grenadiers," in which
the rest would presently join full lustily, waving their long-stemmed pipes
in unison.

So the old fellow would sit, singing
the praises of his scapegrace son,
while his hearers would nod solemn
heads, fostering old Jasper's innocent
delusion for the sake of his white
hairs and the medals upon his
breast.

But now, he was down with "the
rheumatics," and from what Lisbeth
told me when I met her on her way to
and from his cottage, it was rather
more than likely that the high-backed
elbow-chair would know him no more.

Upon the old fellow's illness, Lisbeth

had promptly set herself to see that
he was made comfortable, for Jasper
was a lonely old man—had installed
a competent nurse beside him, and
made it a custom morning and evening to go and see that all was well.

It was for this reason that I sat upon
the Shrubbery gate towards nine
o'clock of a certain evening, swinging
my legs and listening for the sound of
her step along the path. In the ful-
ness of time she came, and getting off
my perch, I took the heavy basket
from her arm, as was usual.

"Dick," she said as we walked on
side by side, "really I'm getting quite
worried about that Imp."

"What has he been up to this time?"
I inquired.

"I'm afraid he must be ill."

"He looked anything but ill yesterday," I answered reassuringly.

"Yes, I know he looks healthy
enough," said Lisbeth, wrinkling her

brows; "but lately he has developed such an enormous appetite. Oh, Dick, it's awful!"

"My poor girl," I retorted, shaking my head, "the genus 'Boy' is distinguished by the two attributes dirt and appetite. You should know that by this time. I myself have harrowing recollections of huge piles of bread and butter, of vast slabs of cake— damp and 'soggy,' and of mysterious hue—of glutinous mixtures purporting to be 'stick-jaw,' one inch of which was warranted to render coherent speech impossible for ten minutes at least. And then the joy of bolting things fiercely in the shade of the pantry, with one's ears on the stretch for foes! I sometimes find myself sighing over the remembrance, even in these days. Don't worry about the Imp's appetite; believe me, it is quite unnecessary."

"Oh, but I can't help it," said Lis-

beth; "it seems somehow so—so
weird. For instance, this morning for
breakfast he had first his usual por-
ridge, then five pieces of bread and
butter, and after that a large slice of
ham—quite a big piece, Dick! And
he ate it all so quickly. I turned away
to ask Jane for the toast, and when I
looked at his plate again it was empty,
he had eaten every bit, and even asked
for more. Of course I refused, so
he tried to get Dorothy to give him
hers in exchange for a broken pocket-
knife. It was just the same at dinner.
He ate the whole leg of a chicken, and
after that a wing, and then some of
the breast, and would have gone on
until he had finished everything, I'm
sure, if I hadn't stopped him, though I
let him eat as long as I dared. Then
at tea he had six slices of bread and
butter, one after the other, not count-
ing toast and cake. He has been like
this for the last two days—and—

oh, yes, cook told me to-night that she found him actually eating dry bread just before he went up to bed. Dry bread—think of it! Oh, Dick, what can be the matter with him?"

"It certainly sounds mysterious," I answered, "especially as regards the dry bread; but that of itself suggests a theory, which, as the detective says in the story, 'I will not divulge just yet;' only don't worry, Lisbeth, the Imp is all right."

Being now come to old Jasper's cottage, which stands a little apart from the village in a by-lane, Lisbeth paused and held out her hand for the basket.

"Don't wait for me to-night," she said. "I ordered Peter to fetch me in the dog-cart; you see, I may be late."

"Is the old chap so very ill?"

"Very, very ill, Dick."

"Poor old Jasper!" I exclaimed.

"Poor old Jasper!" she sighed, and her eyes were brimful of tenderness.

"He is very old and feeble," I said, drawing her close, under pretence of handing her the basket; "and yet with your gentle hand to smooth my pillow, and your eyes to look into mine, I could almost wish——"

"Hush, Dick!"

"Peter or no Peter, I think I'll wait —unless you really wish me to say 'good-night' now?" But with a dexterous turn she eluded me, and waving her hand hurried up the rose-bordered path.

An hour, or even two, does not seem so very long when one's mind is so full of happy thoughts as mine was. Thus, I was filling my pipe and looking philosophically about for a likely spot in which to keep my vigil, when I was aware of a rustling close by, and as I watched a small figure stepped from the shadow of the hedge out into the moonlight.

"Hallo, Uncle Dick!" said a voice.

"Imp!" I exclaimed, "what does this mean? You ought to have been in bed over an hour ago!"

"So I was," he answered with his guileless smile; "only I got up again, you know."

"So it seems!" I nodded.

"An' I followed you an' Auntie Lisbeth all the way, too."

"Did you, though; by George!"

"Yes, an' I dropped one of the parcels an' lost a sausage, but you never heard."

"Lost a sausage!" I repeated, staring.

"Oh, it's all right, you know," he hastened to assure me; "I found it again, an' it wasn't hurt a bit."

"Imp," I said sternly, "come here, I want to talk to you."

"Just a minute, Uncle Dick, while

I get my parcels. I want you to help me to carry them, please," and with the words he dived under the hedge to emerge a moment later with his arms full of unwieldy packages, which he laid at my feet in a row.

"Why, what on earth have you got there, Imp?"

"This," he said, pointing to the first, "is jam an' ham an' a piece of bread; this next one is cakes an' sardines, an' this one is bread-an'-butter that I saved from my tea."

"Quite a collection!" I nodded. "Suppose you tell me what you mean to do with them."

"Well, they're for my outlaw. You remember the other day I wanted to play at being outlaws? Well, two days ago, as I was tracking a base caitiff through the woods with my trusty bow and arrow, I found a real outlaw in the old boat-house."

"Ah! and what is he like?" I inquired.

"Oh, just like an outlaw—only funny, you know, an' most awfull' hungry. Are all outlaws always so very hungry, Uncle Dick?"

"I believe they generally are, Imp. And he looks 'funny,' you say?"

"Yes; I mean his clothes are funny—all over marks like little crosses, only they aren't crosses."

"Like this?" I inquired; and picking up a piece of stick I drew a broad-arrow upon the path.

"Yes, just like that!" cried the Imp in a tone of amazement. "How did you know? You're awfull' clever, Uncle Dick!"

"And he is in the old boat-house, is he?" I said, as I picked up an armful of packages. " 'Lead on, MacDuff!' "

"Mind that parcel, please, Uncle Dick; it's the one I dropped an' lost

the sausage out of—there's one trying
to escape now!"

Having reduced the recalcitrant sausage to a due sense of law and order, we proceeded toward the old
boat-house — a dismal, dismantled
affair, some half mile or so down-
stream.

"And what sort of a fellow is your
outlaw, Imp?"

"Well, I 'spected he'd be awfull'
fierce an' want to hold me for ransom,
but he didn't; he's quite quiet, for an
outlaw, with grey hair and big eyes,
an' eats an awful lot."

"So you saved him your breakfast
and dinner, did you?"

"Oh, yes; an' my tea, too. Auntie
Lisbeth got awfull' angry 'cause she
said I ate too fast; an' Dorothy was
frightened an' wouldn't sit by me
'cause she was 'fraid I'd burst—so
frightfully silly of her!"

"By the way, you didn't tell me what

you have there," I said, pointing to a huge, misshapen, newspaper parcel that he carried beneath one arm.

"Oh, it's a shirt, an' a coat, an' a pair of trousers of Peter's."

"Did Peter give them to you?"

" 'Course not; I took them. You see, my outlaw got tired of being an outlaw, so he asked me to get him some 'togs,' meaning clothes, you know, so I went an' looked in the stable an' found these."

"You don't mean to say that you stole them, Imp?"

" 'Course not!" he answered reproachfully. "I left Peter sixpence an' a note to say I would pay him for them when I got my pocket-money, so help me, Sam!"

"Ah, to be sure!" I nodded.

We were close to the old boat-house now, and upon the Imp's earnest solicitations I handed over my bundles and hid behind a tree, because,

as he pointed out, "his outlaw might
not like me to see him just at first."

Having opened each package with
great care and laid out their contents
upon a log near by, the Imp approached the ruined building with
signs of the most elaborate caution, and
gave three loud, double knocks. Now
casting my eyes about, I espied a
short, heavy stick, and picking it up,
poised it in my hand ready in the
event of possible contingencies.

The situation was decidedly unpleasant, I confess, for I expected nothing
less than to be engaged in a desperate
hand-to-hand struggle within the next
few minutes; therefore, I waited in
some suspense, straining my eyes towards the shadows with my fingers
clasped tight upon my bludgeon.

Then all at once I saw a shape,
ghostly and undefined, flit swiftly
from the gloom of the boat-house,
and next moment a convict was stand-

ing beside the Imp, gaunt and tall
and wild-looking in the moonlight.

His hideous clothes, stained with
mud and the green slime of his hid-
ing-places, hung upon him in tatters,
and his eyes, deep-sunken in his pallid
face, gleamed with an unnatural
brightness as he glanced swiftly about
him—a miserable, hunted creature,
worn by fatigue, and pinched with
want and suffering.

"Did ye get 'em, sonny?" he inquired, in a hoarse, rasping voice.

"Aye, aye, comrade," returned the
Imp; "all's well!"

"Bless ye for that, sonny!" he exclaimed, and with the words he fell
to upon the food, devouring each
morsel as it was handed to him with
a frightful voracity, while his burn-
ing, restless eyes glared about him,
never still for a moment.

Now as I noticed his wasted form
and shaking limbs, I knew that I could

master him with one hand. My weapon
slipped from my slackened grasp, but
at the sound, slight though it was, he
turned and began to run. He had not
gone five yards, however, when he
tripped and fell, and before he could
rise I was standing over him. He
lay there at my feet, perfectly still,
blinking up at me with red-rimmed
eyes.

"All right, master," he said at last;
"you've got me!" But with the
words he suddenly rolled himself towards the river, yet as he struggled to
his knees I pinned him down again.

"Oh, sir! you won't go for to give
me up to them?" he panted. "I've
never done you no wrong. For God's
sake don't send me back to it again,
sir."

" 'Course not," cried the Imp, laying his hand upon my arm; "this is
only Uncle Dick. He won't hurt you,
will you, Uncle Dick?"

"That depends," I answered, keeping tight hold of the tattered coat
collar. "Tell me, what brings you
hanging round here?"

"Used to live up in these parts once,
master."

"Who are you?"

"Convict 49, as broke jail over a
week ago an' would ha' died but for
the little 'un there," and he nodded towards the Imp.

The convict, as I say, was a tall, thin
fellow, with a cadaverous face lined
with suffering, while the hair at his
temples was prematurely white. And
as I looked at him, it occurred to me
that the suffering which had set its
mark so deeply upon him was not
altogether the grosser anguish of the
body. Now for your criminal who can
still feel morally there is surely hope.
I think so, anyhow! For a long moment there was silence, while I stared
into the haggard face below, and the

Imp looked from one to the other of
us, utterly at a loss.

"I wonder if you ever heard tell of
'the bye Jarge,' " I said suddenly.

The convict started so violently that
the jacket tore in my grasp.

"How—how did ye know—?" he
gasped, and stared at me with dropped
jaw.

"I think I know your father."

"My feyther," he muttered; "old
Jasper—'e ain't dead, then?"

"Not yet," I answered; "come, get
up and I'll tell you more while you
eat." Mechanically he obeyed, sitting with his glowing eyes fixed upon
my face the while I told him of old
Jasper's lapse of memory and present
illness.

"Then 'e don't remember as I'm a
thief an' convict 49, master?"

"No; he thinks and speaks of you always as a boy and a pattern son."

The man uttered a strange cry, and

flinging himself upon his knees buried
his face in his hands.

"Come," I said, tapping him on the
shoulder; "take off those things," and
nodding to the Imp, he immediately began unwrapping Peter's garments.

"What, master," cried the convict,
starting up, "are you goin' to let me
see 'im afore you give me up?"

"Yes," I nodded; "only be quick."

In less than five minutes the tattered
prison dress was lying in the bed of
the river, and we were making our
way along the path towards old Jasper's cottage.

The convict spoke but once, and
that as we reached the cottage gate:
"Is he very ill, sir?"

"Very ill," I said. He stood for a
moment, inhaling the fragrance of the
roses in great breaths, and staring
about him; then with an abrupt gesture he opened the little gate, and

gliding up the path with his furtive, stealthy footstep knocked at the door.

For some half hour the Imp and I strolled to and fro in the moonlight, during which he related to me much about his outlaw and the many "ruses he had employed to get him provision." How upon one occasion, to escape the watchful eyes of Auntie Lisbeth, he had been compelled to hide a slice of jam-tart in the trousers-pockets, to the detriment of each; how Dorothy had watched him everywhere in the momentary expectation of "something happening;" how Jane and Peter and cook would stand and stare and shake their heads at him because he ate such a lot, "an' the worst of it was I was awfull' hungry all the time, you know, Uncle Dick!" This and much more he told me as we waited there in the moonlight.

At last the cottage door opened and the convict came out. He did not join

us at once, but remained staring away
towards the river, though I saw him
jerk his sleeve across his eyes more
than once in his furtive, stealthy
fashion; but when at last he came
up to us his face was firm and resolute.

"Did you see old Jasper?" I asked.

"Yes, sir; I saw him."

"Is he any better?"

"Much better—he died in my arms,
sir. An' now I'm ready to go back,
there's a police-station in the village."
He stopped suddenly and turned to
stare back at the lighted windows of
the cottage, and when he spoke again
his voice sounded hoarser than ever.

"Thought I'd come back from fur-
rin parts, 'e did, wi' my pockets stuffed
full o' gold an' bank-notes. Called
me 'is bye Jarge, 'e did!" and again he
brushed his cuff across his eyes.

"Master, I don't know who ye may
be, but I'm grateful to ye an' more

than grateful, sir. An' now I'm ready
to go back an' finish my time."

"How much longer is that?"

"Three years, sir."

"And when you come out, what
shall you do then?"

"Start all over again, sir; try to get
some honest work an' live straight."

"Do you think you can?"

"I know I can, sir. Ye see, he died
in my arms, called me 'is bye Jarge,
said 'e were proud of me, 'e did! A'
man can begin again an' live straight
an' square wi' a memory the like o'
that to 'elp 'im."

"Then why not begin to-night?"

He passed a tremulous hand through
his silver hair, and stared at me with
incredulous eyes.

"Begin—to-night!" he half whispered.

"I have an old house among the
Kentish hop-gardens," I went on;
"no one lives there at present except

a care-taker, but it is within the bounds of probability that I may go to stay there—some day. Now the gardens need trimming, and I'm very fond of flowers; do you suppose you could make the place look decent in—say, a month?"

"Sir," he said in a strange, broken voice, "you ain't jokin' with me, are you?" .

"I could pay you a pound a week; what do you say?"

He tried to speak, but his lips quivered, and he turned his back upon us very suddenly. I tore a page from my pocket-book and scrawled a hasty note to my care-taker.

"Here is the address," I said, tapping him on the shoulder. "You will find no difficulty. I will write again to-night. You must of course have money to get there and may need to buy a few necessaries besides; here is your first week's wages in advance,"

and I thrust a sovereign into his hand.
He stared down at it with blinking
eyes, shuffling awkwardly with his feet,
and at that moment his face seemed
very worn, and lined, and his hair
very grey, yet I had a feeling that I
should not regret my quixotic action
in the end.

"Sir," he faltered, "sir, do ye
mean——?" and stopped.

"I mean that to-night 'the bye Jarge'
has a chance to make a new beginning,
a chance to become the man his father
always thought he would be. Of
course I may be a fool to trust you.
That only time will show; but you see
I had a great respect for old Jasper.
And now that you have the address
you'd better go; stay, though, you
must have a hat; folks might wonder
——take this," and I handed him my
cap.

"Sir, I can't thank ye now, I never
can. It——it won't come; but——"

with a nervous, awkward gesture he caught my hand suddenly, pressed it to his lips, and was gone down the lane.

Thus it was that old Jasper's "bye Jarge" went out to make a trial of life a second time, and as I watched him striding through the moonlight, his head erect, very different to the shambling creature he had been, it seemed to me that the felon was already ousted by the man.

"I 'specks he forgot all 'bout me!" said the Imp disconsolately.

"No," I answered, shaking my head; "I don't think he will ever forget you, my Imp."

"I 'spose he's awfull' fond of you, Uncle Dick?"

"Not that I know of."

"Then why did he kiss your hand?"

"Oh, well—er—perhaps it is a way he has."

"He didn't kiss mine," said the Imp.

A door opened and closed very softly, and Lisbeth came towards us down the path, whereupon the Imp immediately "took cover" in the ditch.

"He is dead, Dick!" she said as I opened the gate. "He died in his son's arms—the George he was always talking about. And oh, Dick, he died trying to sing 'The British Grenadiers.'"

"Poor old Jasper!" I said.

"His son was a convict once, wasn't he?"

"Yes."

"It was strange that he should come back as he did—just in time; it almost seems like the hand of Providence, doesn't it, Dick?"

"Yes." Lisbeth was standing with her elbows upon the gate and her chin in her hands, staring up at the moon, and I saw that her eyes were wet with tears.

"Why, where is your cap?" she ex-

claimed when at last she condescended
to look at me.

"On the head of an escaped convict,"
I answered.

"Do you mean——"

"The 'bye Jarge,' " I nodded.

"Oh, Dick!"

"Yes, Lisbeth; it was a ridiculous
piece of sentiment I admit. Your law-
abiding, level-headed citizen would
doubtless be highly shocked, not to say
scandalised; likewise the Law might
get up on its hind legs and kick—
quite unpleasantly; but all the same, I
did it."

"You were never what one might
call—very 'level-headed,' were you,
Dick?"

"No, I'm afraid not."

"And, do you know, I think that is
the very reason why I—good gracious!—what is that?" She pointed
toward the shadow of the hedge.

"Merely the Imp," I answered;

"but never mind that—tell me what you were going to say—'the very reason why you'—what?"

"Reginald!" said Lisbeth, unheeding my question, "come here, sir!" Very sheepishly the Imp crept forth from the ditch, and coming up beside me, stole his hand into mine, and I put it in my pocket.

"Reginald," she repeated, looking from one to the other of us with that expression which always renews within me the memory of my boyish misdeeds, "why are you not asleep in bed?"

"'Cause I had to go an' feed my outlaw, Auntie Lisbeth."

"And," I put in to create a diversion, "incidentally I've discovered the secret of his 'enormous appetite.' It is explained in three words, to wit, 'the bye Jarge.'"

"Do you mean to say—" began Lisbeth.

"Fed him regularly twice a day," I
went on, "and nearly famished himself in the doing of it—you remember
the dry-bread incident?"

"Imp!" cried Lisbeth; "Imp!" And
she had him next moment in her arms.

"But Uncle Dick gave him a whole
sovereign, you know," he began;
"an'——"

"I sent him to a certain house, Lisbeth," I said, as her eyes met mine;
"an old house that stands not far from
the village of Down, in Kent, to
prune the roses and things. I should
like it to be looking its best when we
get there; and——"

"An' my outlaw kissed Uncle Dick's
hand," pursued the Imp. "Don't you
think he must love him an awful lot?"

"I gave him a month to do it in," I
went on; "but a month seems much
too long when one comes to consider—
what do you think, Lisbeth?"

"I think that I hear the wheels of

the dog-cart!" she cried. Sure enough, a moment later Peter hove in view, and great was his astonishment at sight of "Master Reginald."

"Peter," I said, "Miss Elizabeth has changed her mind, and will walk back with us; and—er—by the way, I understand that Master Reginald purchased a coat, a shirt, and a pair of trousers of you, for which he has already paid a deposit of sixpence. Now, if you will let me know their value——"

"That's hall right, Mr. Brent, sir. Betwixt you and me, sir, they wasn't up to much, nohow, the coat being tightish, sir — tightish — and the trousis uncommon short in the leg for a man o' my hinches, sir."

"Nevertheless," said I, "a coat's a coat, and a pair of trousers are indubitably a pair of trousers, and nothing can alter the fact; so if you will send me in a bill some time I shall be glad."

"Very good, Mr. Brent, sir." Saying which Peter touched his hat and turning, drove away.

"Now," I said as I rejoined Lisbeth and the Imp, "I shall be glad if you will tell me how long it should take for my garden to look fair enough to welcome you?"

"Oh, well, it depends upon the gardener, and the weather, and—and heaps of things," she answered, flashing her dimple at me.

"On the contrary," I retorted, shaking my head, "it depends altogether upon the whim of the most beautiful, tempting——"

"Supposing," sighed Lisbeth, "supposing we talk of fish!"

"You haven't been fishing lately, Uncle Dick," put in the Imp.

"I've had no cause to," I answered; "you see, I am guilty of such things only when life assumes a grey monotony of hue and everything is a flat, dreary desolation. Do you understand, Imp?"

"Not 'zackly—but it sounds fine! Auntie Lisbeth," he said suddenly, as we paused at the Shrubbery gate, "don't you think my outlaw must be very, very fond of Uncle Dick to kiss his hand?"

"Why, of course he must," nodded Lisbeth.

"If," he went on thoughtfully, "if you loved somebody—very much—would you kiss their hand, Auntie Lisbeth?"

"I don't know—of course not!"

"But why not—s'posing their hand was nice an' clean?"

"Oh, well—really I don't know. Imp, run along to bed; do."

"You know now that I wasn't such a pig as to eat all that food, don't you?" Lisbeth kissed him.

"Now be off to bed with you."

"You'll come an' tuck me up, an' kiss me good-night, won't you?"

"To be sure I will," nodded Lisbeth.

"Why, then, I'll go," said the Imp; and with a wave of the hand to me he went.

"Dick," said Lisbeth, staring up at the moon, "it was very unwise of you, to say the least of it, to set a desperate criminal at large."

"I'm afraid it was, Lisbeth; but then I saw there was good in the fellow, you know, and—er——"

"Dick," she said again, and then laughed suddenly, with the dimple in full evidence; "you foolish old Dick— you know you would have done it anyway for the sake of that dying old soldier."

"Poor old Jasper!" I said; "I'm really afraid I should." Then a wonderful thing happened; for as I reached out my hand to her, she caught it suddenly in hers, and before I knew had pressed her lips upon it— and so was gone.

VII

THE BLASTED OAK

I HAD quarrelled with Lisbeth; had quarrelled beyond all hope of redemption and forgiveness, desperately, irrevocably, and it had all come about through a handkerchief—Mr. Selwyn's handkerchief.

At a casual glance this may appear all very absurd, not to say petty; but then I have frequently noticed that insignificant things very often serve for the foundation of great; and incidentally quite a surprising number of lives have been ruined by a handkerchief.

The circumstances were briefly these: In the first place, I had received the following letter from the Duchess, which had perturbed me not a little:

MY DEAR DICK: I hear that that

Agatha Warburton creature has written threatening to cut off our dear
Lisbeth with the proverbial shilling
unless she complies with her wish and
marries Mr. Selwyn within the year.
Did you ever know of anything so dis-
gusting?

If I were Lisbeth, and possessed such
a "creature" for an aunt, I'd see her in
Timbuctoo first—I would! But then,
I forget the poor child has nothing in
the world, and you little more, and
"love in a cottage" is all very well,
Dick, up to a certain time. Of course,
it is all right in novels, but you are
neither of you in a novel, and that is
the worst of it. If Providence had
seen fit to make me Lisbeth's aunt,
now, things might have been very different; but alas! it was not to be. Under the circumstances, the best thing
you can do, for her sake and your
own, is to turn your back upon
Arcadia and try to forget it all as
soon as possible in the swirl of London
and every-day life.

Yours,
CHARLOTTE C.

P.S. Of course, "Romance is dead ages and ages ago; still, it really would be nice if you could manage to run off with her some fine night!

Thus the fiat had gone forth, the time of waiting was accomplished; to-day Lisbeth must choose between Selwyn and myself.

This thought was in my mind as I strode along the river path, filling me with that strange exhilaration which comes, I suppose, to most of us when we face some climax in our lives.

But now the great question, How would she decide? leaped up and began to haunt me. Because a woman smiles upon a man, he is surely a most prodigious fool to flatter himself that she loves him, therefore. How would she decide? Nay, indeed; what choice had she between affluence and penury? Selwyn was wealthy and favoured by her aunt, Lady Warburton, while as for me, my case was altogether the re-

verse. And now I called to mind how
Lisbeth had always avoided coming
to any understanding with me, putting
me off on one pretence or another, but
always with infinite tact. So Fear
came to me, and Doubt began to rear
its head; my step grew slower and
slower, till, reaching the Shrubbery
gate, I leaned there in doubt whether
to proceed or not. Summoning up my
resolution, however, I went on, turning in the direction of the orchard,
where I knew she often sat of a morning to read or make a pretence of sew-
ing.

I had gone but a little way when I
caught sight of two distant figures
walking slowly across the lawn, and
recognised Lisbeth and Mr. Selwyn.

The sight of him here and at such a
time was decidedly unpleasant, and I
hurried on, wondering what could
have brought him so early.

Beneath Lisbeth's favourite tree, an

ancient apple-tree so gnarled and rugged that it seemed to have spent all its days tying itself into all manner of impossible knots—in the shade of this tree, I say, there was a rustic seat and table, upon which was a work-basket, a book, and a handkerchief. It was a large, decidedly masculine handkerchief, and as my eyes encountered it, by some unfortunate chance I noticed a monogram embroidered in one corner—an extremely neat, precise monogram, with the letters F. S. I recognised it at once as the property of Mr. Selwyn.

Ordinarily I should have thought nothing of it, but to-day it was different; for there are times in one's life when the most foolish things become pregnant of infinite possibilities; when the veriest trifles assume overwhelming proportions, filling and blotting out the universe.

So it was now, and as I stared down

at the handkerchief, the Doubt within
me grew suddenly into Certainty.

I was pacing restlessly up and down
when I saw Lisbeth approaching; her
cheeks seemed more flushed than usual,
and her hand trembled as she gave it
to me.

"Why, whatever is the matter with
you?" she said; "you look so—so
strange, Dick."

"I received a letter from the Duchess
this morning."

"Did you?"

"Yes; in which she tells me your
aunt has threatened to——"

"Cut me off with a shilling," nodded
Lisbeth, crossing over to the table.

"Yes," I said again.

"Well?"

"Well?"

"Oh, for goodness' sake, Dick, stop
tramping up and down like a—a caged
bear, and sit down—do!"

I obeyed; yet as I did so I saw her

with the tail of my eye whip up the handkerchief and tuck it beneath the laces at her bosom.

"Lisbeth," said I, without turning my head, "why hide it—there?"

Her face flushed painfully, her lips quivered, and for a moment she could find no answer; then she tried to laugh it off.

"Because I—I wanted to, I suppose!"

"Obviously!" I retorted; and rising, bowed and turned to go.

"Stay a moment, Dick. I have something to tell you."

"Thank you, but I think I can guess."

"Can you?"

"Oh, yes."

"Aren't you just a little bit theatrical, Dick?" Now, as she spoke she drew out Selwyn's handkerchief and began to tie and untie knots in it.

"Dick," she went on—and now she

was tracing out Selwyn's monogram with her finger—"you tell me you know that Aunt Agatha has threatened to disinherit me; can you realise what that would mean to me, I wonder?"

"Only in some small part," I answered bitterly; "but it would be awful for you, of course—good-bye to society and all the rest of it—no more ball gowns or hats and things from Paris, and——"

"And bearing all this in mind," she put in, "and knowing me as you do, perhaps you can make another guess and tell me what I am likely to do under these circumstances?"

Now, had I been anything but a preposterous ass, my answer would have been different; but then I was not myself, and I could not help noticing how tenderly her finger traced out those two letters F. S., so I laughed rather brutally and answered:

"Follow the instinct of your sex and
stick to the Paris hats and things."

I heard her breath catch, and turning
away, she began to flutter the pages
of the book upon the table.

"And you were always so clever at
guessing, weren't you?" she said after
a moment, keeping her face averted.

"At least it has saved your explain-
ing the situation, and you should be
thankful for that."

The book slipped suddenly to the
ground and lay, all unheeded, and she
began to laugh in a strange, high key.
Wondering, I took a step toward her;
but as I did so she fled from me, running toward the house, never stopping
or slackening speed, until I had lost
sight of her altogether.

Thus the whole miserable business
had befallen, dazing me by its very
suddenness like a "bolt from the blue."
I had returned to the 'Three Jolly
Anglers,' determined to follow the ad-

vice of the Duchess and return to London by the next train. Yet, after passing a sleepless night, here I was sitting in my old place beneath the alders pretending to fish.

The river was laughing among the reeds just as merrily as ever, bees hummed and butterflies wheeled and hovered—life and the world were very fair. Yet for once I was blind to it all; moreover, my pipe refused to "draw"—pieces of grass, twigs, and my penknife were alike unavailing.

So I sat there, brooding upon the fickleness of womankind, as many another has done before me, and many will doubtless do after, alack!

And the sum of my thoughts was this: Lisbeth had deceived me; the hour of trial had found her weak; my idol was only common clay, after all. And yet she had but preferred wealth to comparative poverty, which surely, according to all the rules of common

MY LADY CAPRICE

sense, had shown her possessed of a
wisdom beyond her years. And who
was I to sit and grieve over it? Under the same circumstances ninety-nine
women out of a hundred would have
chosen precisely the same course; but
then to me Lisbeth had always seemed
the one exempt—the hundredth woman; moreover, there be times when
love, unreasoning and illogical, is infinitely more beautiful than this much-
vaunted common sense.

This and much more was in my mind
as I sat fumbling with my useless pipe
and staring with unseeing eyes at the
flow of the river. My thoughts, however, were presently interrupted by
something soft rubbing against me,
and looking down, I beheld Dorothy's
fluffy kitten Louise. Upon my at-
tempting to pick her up, she bounded
from me in that remarkable sideways
fashion peculiar to her kind, and stood
regarding me from a distance, her tail

straight up in the air and her mouth opening and shutting without a sound. At length, having given vent to a very feeble attempt at a mew, she zigzagged to me, and climbing upon my knee, immediately fell into a purring slumber.

"Hallo, Uncle Dick!—I mean, what ho, Little John!" cried a voice, and looking over my shoulder, carefully so as not to disturb the balance of "Louise," I beheld the Imp. It needed but a glance at the bow in his hand, the three arrows in his belt, and the feather in his cap, to tell me who he was for the time being.

"How now, Robin?" I inquired.

"I'm a bitter, disappointed man, Uncle Dick!" he answered, putting up a hand to feel if his feather was in place.

"Are you?"

"Yes; the book says that Robin Hood

was 'bitter an' disappointed,' an' so am I!"

"Why, how's that?"

The Imp folded his arms and regarded me with a terrific frown.

"It's all the fault of my Auntie Lisbeth!" he said in a tragic voice.

"Sit down, my Imp, and tell me all about it."

"Well," he began, laying aside his 'trusty sword,' and seating himself at my elbow, "she got awfull' angry with me yesterday, awfull' angry, indeed, an' she wouldn't play with me or anything; an' when I tried to be friends with her an' asked her to pretend she was a hippopotamus, 'cause I was a mighty hunter, you know, she just said, 'Reginald, go away an' don't bother me!' "

"You surprise me, Imp!"

"But that's not the worst of it," he continued, shaking his head gloomily; "she didn't come to 'tuck me up' an'

kiss me good-night like she always
does. I lay awake hours an' hours
waiting for her, you know; but she
never came, an' so I've left her!"

"Left her!" I repeated.

"For ever an' ever!" he said, nodding a stern brow. "I 'specks she'll
be awfull' sorry some day!"

"But where shall you go to?"

"I'm thinking of Persia!" he said
darkly.

"Oh!"

"It's nice an' far, you know, an' I
might meet Aladdin with the wonderful lamp."

"Alas, Imp, I fear not," I answered,
shaking my head; "and besides, it will
take a long, long time to get there, and
where shall you sleep at night?"

The Imp frowned harder than ever,
staring straight before him as one who
wrestles with some mighty problem,
then his brow cleared and he spoke in
this wise:

"Henceforth, Uncle Dick, my roof shall be the broad expanse of heaven, an'—an'—wait a minute!" he broke off, and lugging something from his pocket, disclosed a tattered, paper-covered volume (the Imp's books are always tattered), and hastily turning the pages, paused at a certain paragraph and read as follows:

" 'Henceforth my roof shall be the broad expanse of heaven, an' all tyrants shall learn to tremble at my name!' Doesn't that sound fine, Uncle Dick? I tried to get Ben—you know, the gardener's boy—to come an' live in the 'greenwood' with me a bit an' help to make 'tyrants' tremble, but he said he was 'fraid his mother might find him some day, an' he wouldn't, so I'm going to make them tremble all by myself, unless you will come an' be Little John, like you were once before—oh, do!"

Before I could answer, hearing footsteps, I looked round, and my heart leaped, for there was Lisbeth coming down the path.

Her head was drooping and she walked with a listless air. Now, as I watched I forgot everything but that she looked sad, and troubled, and more beautiful than ever, and that I loved her. Instinctively I rose, lifting my cap. She started, and for the fraction of a second her eyes looked into mine, then she passed serenely on her way. I might have been a stick or stone for all the further notice she bestowed.

Side by side, the Imp and I watched her go, until the last gleam of her white skirt had vanished amid the green. Then he folded his arms and turned to me.

"So be it!" he said, with an air of stern finality; "an' now, what is a 'blasted oak,' please?"

"A blasted oak!" I repeated.

"If you please, Uncle Dick."

"Well, it's an oak-tree that has been struck by lightning."

"Like the one with the 'stickie-out' branches, where I once hid Auntie Lis—Her stockings?"

I nodded, and sitting down, began to pack up my fishing rod and things.

"I'm glad of that," pursued the Imp thoughtfully. "Robin Hood was always saying to somebody, 'Hie thee to the blasted oak at midnight!' an' it's nice to have one handy, you know."

I thought that under certain circumstances, and with a piece of rope, it would be very much so, "blasted" or otherwise, but I only said, "Yes" and sighed.

" 'Whence that doleful visage,' Uncle Dick—I mean Little John? Is Auntie angry with you, too?"

"Yes," I answered, and sighed again.

"Oh!" said the Imp, staring, "an' do you feel like—like—wait a minute"—

and once more he drew out and consulted the tattered volume—" 'do you feel like hanging yourself in your sword-belt to the arm of yonder tree?' " he asked eagerly, with his finger upon a certain paragraph.

"Very like it, my Imp."

"Or—or 'hurling yourself from the topmost pinnacle of yon lofty crag?' "

"Yes, Imp; the 'loftier' the better!"

"Then you must be in love, like Alan-a-Dale; he was going to hang himself, an' 'hurl himself off the topmost pinnacle,' you know, only Robin Hood said, 'Whence that doleful visage,' an' stopped him—you remember?"

"To be sure," I nodded.

"An' so you are really in love with my Auntie Lis—Her, are you?"

"Yes."

"Is that why she's angry with you?"

"Probably."

The Imp was silent, apparently plunged once more in a profound meditation.

"'Fraid there's something wrong with her," he said at last, shaking his head; "she's always getting angry with everybody 'bout something—you an' me an' Mr. Selwyn——"

"Mr. Selwyn!" I exclaimed. "Imp, what do you mean?"

"Well, she got cross with me first—an' over such a little thing, too! We were in the orchard, an' I spilt some lemonade on her gown—only about half a glass, you know, an' when she went to wipe it off she hadn't a handkerchief, an' 'course I had none. So she told me to fetch one, an' I was just going when Mr. Selwyn came, so I said, 'Would he lend Auntie Lisbeth his handkerchief, 'cause she wanted one to wipe her dress?' an' he said, 'Delighted!' Then auntie frowned at me an' shook her head when he wasn't looking. But Mr. Selwyn took out his handkerchief, an' got down on his knees, an' began to wipe off the lemonade, telling her something 'bout his 'heart,' an' wishing he could 'kneel at her feet forever!' Auntie got awfull' red, an' told him to stand up, but he wouldn't; an' then she looked at me so awfull' cross that I thought I'd better leave, so while she was saying, 'Rise, Mr. Selwyn—do!' I ran away, only I could tell she was awfull' angry with Mr. Selwyn—an' that's all!"

I rose to my knees and caught the Imp by the shoulders.

"Imp," I cried, "are you sure—quite sure that she was angry with Mr. Selwyn yesterday morning?"

"'Course I am. I always know when Auntie Lisbeth's angry. An' now let's go an' play at 'Blasted Oaks.'"

"Anything you like, Imp, so long as we find her."

"You're forgetting your fishing rod an'——"

"Fishing rod be—blowed!" I exclaimed, and set off hurriedly in the direction Lisbeth had taken.

The Imp trotted beside me, stumbling frequently over his "trusty sword" and issuing numberless commands in a hoarse, fierce voice to an imaginary "band of outlaws." As for me, I strode on unheeding, for my mind was filled with a fast-growing suspicion that I had judged Lisbeth like a hasty fool.

In this manner we scoured the neighbourhood very thoroughly, but with no success. However, we continued our search with unabated ardour—along the river path to the water stairs and from thence by way of the gardens to the orchard; but not a sign of Lisbeth. The shrubbery and paddock yielded a like result, and having interrogated Peter in the harness-room, he informed us that "Miss Helezabeth was hout along with Miss Dorothy."

At last, after more than an hour of this sort of thing, even the Imp grew discouraged and suggested "turning pirates."

Our wanderings had led by devious paths, and now, as luck would have it, we found ourselves beneath "the blasted oak."

We sat down very solemnly side by side, and for a long time there was silence.

"It's fine to make 'tyrants tremble,' isn't it, Uncle Dick?" said the Imp at last.

"Assuredly," I nodded.

"But I should have liked to kiss Auntie Lisbeth good-bye first, an' Dorothy, an' Louise——"

"What do you mean, my Imp?"

"Oh, you know, Uncle Dick! 'My roof henceforth shall be the broad expanse.' I'm going to fight giants an'

—an' all sorts of cads, you know. An'
then, if ever I get to Persia an' do
find the wonderful lamp, I can wish
everything all right again, an' we
should all be 'happy ever after'—you
an' Auntie Lisbeth an' Dorothy an'
me; an' we could live in a palace with
slaves. Oh, it would be fine!"

"Yes, it's an excellent idea, Imp, but
on the whole slightly risky, because
it's just possible that you might never
find the lamp; besides, you'll have to
stop here, after all, because, you see,
I'm going away myself."

"Then let's go away together, Uncle
Dick, do!"

"Impossible, my Imp; who will look
after your Auntie Lisbeth and Dorothy and Louise?"

"I forgot that," he answered rue-
fully.

"And they need a deal of taking care
of," I added.

"'Fraid they do," he nodded; "but

there's Peter," he suggested, brightening.

"Peter certainly knows how to look after horses, but that is not quite the same. Lend me your 'trusty sword.' "

He rose, and drawing it from his belt, handed it to me with a flourish.

"You remember in the old times, Imp, when knights rode out to battle, it was customary for them when they made a solemn promise to kiss the cross-hilt of their swords, just to show they meant to keep it. So now I ask you to go back to your Auntie Lisbeth, to take care of her, to shield and guard her from all things evil, and never to forget that you are her loyal and true knight; and now kiss your sword in token, will you?" and I passed back the weapon.

"Yes," he answered, with glistening eyes, "I will, on my honour, so help me Sam!" and he kissed the sword.

"Good!" I exclaimed; "thank you, Imp."

"But are you really going away?" he inquired, looking at me with a troubled face.

"Yes!"

"Must you go?"

"Yes."

"Will you promise to come back some day—soon?"

"Yes, I promise."

"On your honour?"

"On my honour!" I repeated, and in my turn I obediently kissed his extended sword-hilt.

"Are you going to-night, Uncle Dick?"

"I start very early in the morning, so you see we had better say 'good-bye' now, my Imp."

"Oh!" he said, and stared away down the river. Now, in the button-hole of my coat there hung a fading rosebud which Lisbeth had given me

two days ago, and acting on impulse,
I took it out.

"Imp," I said, "when you get back,
I want you to give this to your
Auntie Lisbeth and say—er—never
mind, just give it to her, will
you?"

"Yes, Uncle Dick," he said, taking
it from me, but keeping his face turned
away.

"And now good-bye, Imp!"

"Good-bye!" he answered, still without looking at me.

"Won't you shake hands?"

He thrust out a grimy little palm,
and as I clasped it I saw a big tear roll
down his cheek.

"You'll come back soon—very soon
—Uncle Dick?"

"Yes, I'll come back, my Imp."

"So—help you—Sam?"

"So help me Sam!"

And thus it was we parted, the Imp
and I, beneath the "blasted oak," and

I know my heart was strangely heavy as I turned away and left him.

After I had gone some distance I paused to look back. He still stood where I had left him, but his face was hidden in his arms as he leaned sobbing against the twisted trunk of the great tree.

All the way to the 'Three Jolly Anglers' and during the rest of the evening the thought of the little desolate figure haunted me, so much so that, having sent away my dinner untasted, I took pen and ink and wrote him a letter, enclosing with it my penknife, which I had often seen him regard with "the eye of desire," despite the blade he had broken upon a certain memorable occasion. This done, I became possessed of a determination to send some message to Lisbeth also— just a few brief words which should yet reveal to her something of the

thoughts I bore her ere I passed out
of her life forever.

For over an hour I sat there, chew-
ing the stem of my useless pipe and
racking my brain, but the "few brief
words" obstinately refused to come.

Nine o'clock chimed mournfully
from the Norman tower of the church
hard by, yet still my pen was idle and
the paper before me blank; also I became conscious of a tapping somewhere close at hand, now stopping,
now beginning again, whose weari-
some iteration so irritated my frac-
tious nerves that I flung down my pen
and rose.

The noise seemed to come from the
vicinity of the window. Crossing to
it, therefore, I flung the casement suddenly open, and found myself staring
into a round face, in which were set
two very round eyes and a button of a
nose, the whole surmounted by a shock
of red hair.

"'Allo, Mr. Uncle Dick!"

It needed but this and a second glance at the round face to assure me that it pertained to Ben, the gardener's boy.

"What, my noble Benjamin?" I exclaimed.

"No, it's me!" answered the redoubtable Ben. "'E said I was to give you this an' tell you, 'Life an' death!'" As he spoke he held out a roll of paper tied about the middle with a boot lace; which done, the round head grinned, nodded, and disappeared from my ken. Unwinding the boot lace, I spread out the paper and read the following words, scrawled in pencil:

Hi the to the Blarsted Oke and all will be forgiven. Come back to your luving frends and bigones shall be bigones. Look to the hole in the trunk there of.

Sined,

Robin, Outlaw and Knight.

P.S. I mean where i hid her stockings—you no.

I stood for some time with this truly
mysterious document in my hand, in
two minds what to do about it; if I
went, the chances were that I should
run against the Imp, and there would
be a second leave-taking, which in my
present mood I had small taste for.
On the other hand, there was a possi-
bility that something might have
transpired which I should do well to
know.

And yet what more could transpire?
Lisbeth had made her choice, my
dream was over, to-morrow I should
return to London—and there was an
end of it all; still——

In this pitiful state of vacillation I
remained for some time, but in the end
curiosity and a fugitive hope gained
the day, and taking my cap, I sallied
forth.

It was, as Stevenson would say, "a

wonderful night of stars," and the air was full of their soft, quivering light, for the moon was late and had not risen as yet. As I stepped from the inn door, somebody in the tap-room struck up "Tom Bowling" in a rough but not unmusical voice; and the plaintive melody seemed somehow to become part of the night.

Truly, my feet trod a path of "faerie," carpeted with soft mosses, a path winding along beside a river of shadows on whose dark tide stars were floating. I walked slowly, breathing the fragrance of the night and watching the great, silver moon creeping slowly up the spangled sky. So I presently came to the "blasted oak." The hole in the trunk needed little searching for. I remembered it well enough, and thrusting in my hand, drew out a folded paper. Holding this close to my eyes, I managed with no little difficulty to decipher this message:

Don't go unkel dick bekors Auntie
lisbeth wants you and i want you to.
I heard her say so to herself in the
libree and she was crying to, and
didn't see me there but i was. And
she said O Dick i want you so, out
loud bekors she didn't no I was there.
And i no she was crying bekors i saw
the tiers. And this is true on my
onner so help me sam.
Sined,
Yore true frend and Knight,
REGINALD AUGUSTUS.

A revulsion of feeling swept over me
as I read. Ah! if only I could believe
she had said such words—my beautiful, proud Lisbeth.

Alas! dear Imp, how was it possible
to believe you? And because I knew
it could not possibly be true, and because I would have given my life to
know that it *was* true, I began to read
the note all over again.

Suddenly I started and looked
round; surely that was a sob! But the

moon's level rays served only to show the utter loneliness about me. It was imagination, of course, and yet it had sounded very real.

And she said, "O Dick, I want you so!"

The river lapped softly against the bank, and somewhere above my head the leaves rustled dismally.

"Dear little Imp, if it were only true!"

Once again the sound came to me, low and restrained, but a sob unmistakably.

On the other side of the giant tree I beheld a figure half sitting, half lying. The shadow was deep here, but as I stooped the kindly moon sent down a shaft of silver light, and I saw a lovely, startled face, with great, tear-dimmed eyes.

"Lisbeth!" I exclaimed; then,

prompted by a sudden thought, I glanced hastily around.

"I am alone," she said, interpreting my thought aright.

"But—here—and—and at such an hour!" I stammered foolishly. She seemed to be upon her feet in one movement, fronting me with flashing eyes.

"I came to look for the Imp. I found this on his pillow. Perhaps you will explain?" and she handed me a crumpled paper.

DEAR AUNTIE LISBATH: (I read) Unkel dick is going away bekors he is in luv with you and you are angry with the Blarsted oke, where I hid yore stokkings if you want to kiss me and be kind to me again, come to me bekors I want someboddie to be nice to me now he is gone.

yore luving sorry IMP.
P.S. He said he would like to hang himself in his sword-belt to the arm of yonder tree and hurl himself from

yon topmost pinnakel, so I no he is in
luv with you.

"Oh, blessed Imp!"

"And now where is he?" she demanded.

"Lisbeth, I don't know."

"You don't know! Then why are
you here?"

For answer I held out the letter I had
found, and watched while she read the
words I could not believe.

Her hat was off, and the moon made
wonderful lights in the coils of her
black hair. She was wearing an in-
door gown of some thin material that
clung, boldly revealing the gracious
lines of her supple figure, and in the
magic of the moon she seemed some
young goddess of the woods—tall and
fair and strong, yet infinitely womanly.

Now as she finished reading she
turned suddenly away, yet not before
I had seen the tell-tale colour glowing
in her cheeks—a slow wave which

surged over her from brow to chin, and chin to the round, white column of her throat.

And she said, "O Dick, I want you so!" I read aloud.

"Oh," Lisbeth murmured.

"Lisbeth, is it true?"

She stood with her face averted, twisting the letter in her fingers.

"Lisbeth!" I said, and took a step nearer. Still she did not speak, but her hands came out to me with a swift, passionate gesture, and her eyes looked into mine; and surely none were ever more sweet, with the new shyness in their depths and the tears glistening on their lashes.

And in that moment Doubt and Fear were swallowed up in a great joy, and I forgot all things save that Lisbeth was before me and that I loved her.

The moon, risen now, had made a broad path of silver across the shad-

owy river to our very feet, and I remembered how the Imp had once told
me that it was there for the moon
fairies to come down by when they
bring us happy dreams. Surely, the
air was full of moon fairies to-
night.

"O Imp, thrice blessed Imp!"

"But—but Selwyn?" I groaned at
last.

"Well?"

"If you love him——"

"But I don't!"

"But if you are to marry him——"

"But I'm not! I was going to tell
you so in the orchard yesterday, but
you gave me no chance; you preferred
to guess, and, of course, guessed
wrong altogether. I knew it made
you wretched, and I was glad of it and
meant to keep you so a long, long
time; but when I looked up and saw
you standing there so very, very miserable, Dick, I couldn't keep it up any

longer, because I was so dreadfully wretched myself, you know."

"Can you ever forgive me?"

"That depends, Dick."

"On what?"

Lisbeth stooped, and picking up her hat, began to put it on.

"Depends on what?" I repeated.

Her hat was on now, but for a while she did not answer, her eyes upon the "fairy path." When at last she spoke her voice was very low and tender.

" 'Not far from the village of Down, in Kent, there is a house,' " she began, " 'a very old house, with pointed gables and pannelled chambers, but empty to-night and desolate.' You see I remember it all," she broke off.

"Yes, you remember it all," I repeated, wondering.

"Dick—I—I want you to—take me there. I've thought of it all so often. Take me there, Dick."

"Lisbeth, do you mean it?"

"It has been the dream of my life for a long time now—to work for you there, to take care of you, Dick—you need such a deal, such a great deal of taking care of—to walk with you in the old rose garden; but I'm a beggar now, you know, though I sha'n't mind a bit if—if you want me, Dick."

"Want you!" I cried, and with the words I drew her close and kissed her.

Now, from somewhere in the tree above came a sudden crack and mighty snapping of twigs.

"All right, Uncle Dick!" cried a voice; "it's only the branch. Don't worry."

"Imp!" I exclaimed.

"I'm coming, Uncle Dick," he answered, and with much exertion and heavy breathing he presently emerged into view and squirmed himself safely to earth. For a moment he stood looking from one to the other of us, then he turned to Lisbeth.

"Won't you forgive me, too, Auntie Lisbeth, please?" he said.

"Forgive you!" she cried, and falling on her knees, gathered him in her arms.

"I'm glad I didn't go to Persia, after all, Uncle Dick," he said over her shoulder.

"Persia!" repeated Lisbeth, wonderingly.

"Oh, yes; you were so angry with Uncle Dick an' me—so frightfull' angry, you know, that I was going to try to find the 'wonderful lamp' so I could wish everything all right again an' all of us 'live happy ever after'; but the blasted oak did just as well, an' was nicer, somehow, wasn't it?"

"Infinitely nicer," I answered.

"An' you will never. be angry with Uncle Dick or me any more, will you, auntie—that is, not frightfull' angry, you know?"

"Never any more, dear."

"On your honour?"

"On my honour!"

"So help you Sam?"

"So help me Sam!" she repeated, smiling, but there were tears in her voice.

Very gravely the Imp drew his "trusty sword," which she, following his instructions, obediently kissed.

"And now," cried he, "we are all happy again, aren't we?"

"More happy than I ever hoped or dreamed to be," answered Lisbeth, still upon her knees; "and oh, Imp—dear little Imp, come and kiss me."

VIII

THE LAND OF HEART'S DELIGHT

SURELY there never was and never
could be such another morning as this!
Ever since the first peep of dawn a
blackbird had been singing to me from
the fragrant syringa-bush that blos-
somed just beneath my window. Each
morning I had wakened to the joyous
melody of his golden song. But to-
day the order was reversed. I had sat
there at my open casement, breathing
the sweet purity of the morning,
watching the eastern sky turn slowly
from pearl-grey to saffron and from
saffron to deepest crimson, until at last
the new-risen sun had filled all the
world with his glory. And then this
blackbird of mine had begun—very
hoarse at first, trying a note now and

then in a tentative sort of fashion, as
though still drowsy and not quite sure
of himself, but little by little his notes
had grown longer, richer, mellower,
until here he was pouring out his soul
in an ecstasy.

Ah! surely there never was, there
never could be, such another morning
as this!

Out of the green twilight of the
woods a gentle wind was blowing,
laden with the scent of earth and hidden flowers. Dewdrops twinkled in
the grass and hung glistening from
every leaf and twig, and beyond all
was the sheen of the murmurous
river.

The blackbird was in full song now,
and by degrees others joined in—
thrush, and lark, and linnet, with the
humbler voices of the farmyard—until the sunny air was vibrant with the
chorus.

Presently a man in a sleeved waistcoat crossed the paddock, whistling lustily, and from somewhere below there rose a merry clatter of plates and dishes; and thus the old inn, which had seen so many mornings, woke up to yet another.

But there never was, there never could be, just such another morning as this was!

And in a little while, having dressed with more than usual care, I went downstairs to find my breakfast awaiting me in the "Sanded Parlour," having ordered it for this early hour the night previously—ham and eggs and fragrant coffee, what mortal could wish for more?

And while I ate, waited on by the rosy-cheeked chambermaid, in came Master Amos Baggett, mine host, to pass the time of day, and likewise to assure me that my baggage should catch the early train; who when I rose, my meal at an end, paused to wipe his honest hand quite needlessly upon his snowy apron ere he wished me "Good-bye."

So having duly remembered the aforesaid rosy-cheeked chambermaid, the obsequious "Boots" and the grinning ostler, I sallied forth into the sunshine, and crossing the green, where stood the battered sign-post, I came to a flight of rough steps, at the foot of which my boat was moored. In I stepped, cast loose the painter, and shipping the sculls, shot out into the stream.

No, there never was, there never could be, just such another morning as this, for to-day I was to marry Lisbeth, and every stroke of the oar carried me nearer to her and happiness.

Gaily the alders bent and nodded to me; joyfully the birds piped and sang; merrily the water laughed and chattered against my prow as I rowed through the golden morning.

MY LADY CAPRICE

Long before the hour appointed I
reached the water-stairs at Fane
Court, and tying my skiff, lighted my
pipe and watched the smoke rise
slowly into the still air while I tried
"to possess my soul in patience."

Sitting thus, I deamed many a fair
dream of the new life that was to be,
and made many resolutions, as a man
should upon his wedding morn.

And at last came Lisbeth herself,
swiftly, lightly, as fair and sweet and
fresh as the morning, who yet paused
a while to lean upon the balustrade
and look down at me beneath the brim
of her hat. Up I rose and stretched
out my hands to her, but she still stood
there, and I saw her cheeks were
flushed and her eyes shy and tender.

So once more we stood upon the old
water-stairs, she on the top stair, I on
the lower; and again I saw the little
foot beneath her skirt come slowly
towards me and hesitate.

"Again I saw the little foot
beneath her skirt come slowly
towards me and hesitate"

"Dick," she said, "you know that Aunt Agatha has cut me off—disinherited me altogether—you have had time to think it all over?"

"Yes."

"And you are quite—quite sure?"

"Quite! I think I have been so all my life."

"I'm penniless now, Dick, a beggar, with nothing in the world but the clothes I wear."

"Yes," I said, catching her hands in mine, "my beggar-maid; the loveliest, noblest, sweetest that ever stooped to bestow her love on man."

"Dick, how glorious everything is this morning—the earth, the sky, and the river!"

"It is our wedding morning!" said I.

"Our wedding day," she repeated in a whisper.

"And there never was just such a morning as this," said I.

"But, Dick, all days cannot be as

this—there must come clouds and
storm sometimes, and—and—O Dick!
are you sure that you will never, never
regret———"

"I love you, Lisbeth, in the shadow
as well as the sunshine—love you ever
and always." And so, the little foot
hesitating no longer, Lisbeth came
down to me.

Oh, never again could there be such
another morning as this!

"Ahoy!"

I looked round with a start, and
there, his cap cocked rakishly over one
eye, his "murderous cutlass" at his hip
and his arms folded across his chest,
stood "Scarlet Sam, the Terror of the
South Seas."

"Imp!" cried Lisbeth.

"Avast!" cried he in lusty tones;
"whereaway?"

I glanced helplessly at Lisbeth and
she at me.

"Whereaway, shipmate?" he bellowed in nautical fashion, but before I could find a suitable answer Dorothy made her appearance with the fluffy kitten "Louise" cuddled under her arm as usual.

"How do you do?" she said demurely; "it's awfully nice to get up so early, isn't it? We heard auntie creeping about on tippity-toes, you know, so we came, too. Reginald said she was pretending to be burglars, but I think she's going 'paddling.' Are you, auntie?"

"No, dear; not this morning," answered Lisbeth, shaking her head.

"Then you are going for a row in Uncle Dick's boat. How fine!"

"An' you'll take us with you, won't you, Uncle Dick?" cried the Imp eagerly. "We'll be pirates. I'll be 'Scarlet Sam,' an' you can be 'Timothy Bone, the bo'sun,' like you were last time."

"Impossible, my Imp," I said firmly.

He looked at me incredulously for a moment, then, seeing I meant it, his lip began to quiver.

"I didn't think 'T-Timothy B-Bone' would ever desert me," he said, and turned away.

"Oh, auntie!" exclaimed Dorothy, "won't you take us?"

"Dear—not this morning."

"Are you going far, then, Uncle Dick?"

"Yes, very far," I answered, glancing uneasily from the Imp's drooping figure to Lisbeth.

"I wonder where?"

"Oh—well—er—down the river," I stammered, quite at a loss.

"Y-e-s, but where?" persisted Dorothy.

"Well, to—er—to——"

"To the 'Land of Heart's Delight,'" Lisbeth put in, "and you may come with us, after all, if Uncle Dick will take you."

"To be sure he will, if your auntie wishes it," I cried, "so step aboard, my hearties, and lively!" In a moment the Imp's hand was in mine, and he was smiling up at me with wet lashes.

"I knew 'Timothy Bone' could never be a—a 'mutinous rogue,'" he said, and turned to aid Dorothy aboard with the air of an admiral on his flagship.

And now, all being ready, he unhitched the painter, or, as he said, "slipped our cable," and we glided out into midstream.

"A ship," he said thoughtfully, "always has a name. What shall we call this one? Last time we were 'pirates' and she was the *Black Death*——"

"Never mind last time, Imp," I broke in; "to-day she is the *Joyful Hope.*"

"That doesn't sound very 'pirate-y,' somehow," he responded with a dis-

paraging shake of the head, "but I
s'pose it will have to do."

And so, upon that summer morning,
the good ship *Joyful Hope* set sail for
the "Land of Heart's Delight," and
surely no vessel of her size ever carried quite such a cargo of happiness
before or since.

And once again "Scarlet Sam"
stamped upon the "quarter-deck" and
roared orders anent "lee shrouds" and
"weather braces," with divers injunc-
tions concerning the "helm," while his
eyes rolled and he flourished his "murderous cutlass" as he had done upon a
certain other memorable occasion.

Never, never again could there be
just such another morning as this—
for two of us at least.

On we went, past rush and sedge and
weeping willow, by roaring weir and
cavernous lock, into the shadow of
grim stone bridges and out again into
the sunshine, past shady woods and

green uplands, until at length we "cast anchor" before a flight of steps leading up to a particularly worn stone gateway surmounted by a crumbling stone cross.

"Why," exclaimed the Imp, staring, "this is a church!"

"Imp," I nodded, "I believe it is."

"But to-day isn't Sunday, you know," he remonstrated, seeing it was our intention to land.

"Never mind that, Imp; 'the better the deed, the better the day, you know.' "

On we went, Dorothy with the fluffy Louise beneath her arm and the Imp with cutlass swinging at his belt, while Lisbeth and I brought up the rear, and as we went she slipped her hand into mine. In the porch we came upon an aged woman busy with a broom and a very large duster, who, catching sight of Dorothy's kitten and the Imp's "murderous weapon," dropped first the duster and then the broom, and stood staring in open-mouthed astonishment.

And there in the dim old church, with the morning sun making a glory of the window above our heads, and with the birds for our choristers, the vows were exchanged and the blessing pronounced that gave Lisbeth and her future into my keeping; yet I think we were both conscious of those two small figures in the gloom of the great pew behind, who stared in round-eyed wonderment.

The register duly signed, and all formalities over and done, we go out into the sunshine; and once more the aged woman, richer now by half a crown, is reduced to mute astonishment, so that speech is beyond her, when the Imp, lifting his feathered cap, politely wishes her "good-morning."

Being come aboard the *Joyful Hope,* there ensued an awkward pause, during which Lisbeth looked at the children and I at her.

"We must take them back home," she said at last.

"We shall miss our train, Lisbeth."

"But," and here she blushed most delightfully, "there is really no hurry; we can take a—a later one."

"So be it," I said, and laid our course accordingly.

For a time there was silence, during which the Imp, as if in momentary expectation of an attack by bloodthirsty foes, scowled about him, pistol in hand, keeping, as he said, "his weather eye lifting," while Dorothy glanced from Lisbeth to me and back again with puzzled brows.

"I do believe you have been marrying each other!" she said suddenly. The Imp forgot all about his "weather eye" and stared aghast.

"'Course not!" he cried at last.

"Uncle Dick wouldn't do such a thing, would you, Uncle Dick?"

"Imp, I have—I do confess it."

"Oh!" he exclaimed in a tone of deepest tragedy. "And you let him go and do it, Auntie Lisbeth?"

"He was so very, very persistent, Imp," she said, actually turning crimson beneath his reproachful eye.

"Don't be too hard on us, Imp," I pleaded.

"I s'pose it can't be helped now," he said, a little mollified, but frowning sternly, nevertheless.

"No," I answered, with my eyes upon Lisbeth's lovely, blushing face, "it certainly can't be helped now."

"And you'll never do it again?"

"Never again, Imp."

"Then I forgive you, only why—why did you do it?"

"Well, you see, my Imp, I have an old house in the country, a very cosy old place, but it's lonely, horribly lonely, to live by one's self. I've wanted somebody to help me to live in it for a long time, but nobody would, you know, Imp. At last your Auntie Lisbeth has promised to take care of the house and me, to fill the desolate rooms with her voice and sweet presence, and my empty life with her life. You can't quite understand how much this means to me now, Imp, but you will some day, perhaps."

"But are you going to take our Auntie Lisbeth away from us?" cried Dorothy.

"Yes, dear," I answered, "but——"

"Oh, I don't like that one bit!" exclaimed the Imp.

"But you shall come there and stay with us as often as you wish," said Lisbeth.

"That would be perfectly beautiful!" cried Dorothy.

"Yes, but when?" inquired the Imp gloomily.

"Soon," I answered.

"Very soon!" said Lisbeth.

"Will you promise to be 'Timothy Bone, the bo'sun,' an' the 'Black Knight,' an' 'Little-John' whenever I want you to—so help you Sam, Uncle Dick?"

"I will, Imp."

"An' make me a long sword with a— a 'deadly point'?"

"Yes," I nodded, "and show you some real ones, too."

"Real ones?" he cried.

"Oh, yes, and armour as well; there's lots of it in the old house, you know."

"Let's go now!" he cried, nearly upsetting the boat in his eagerness.

"Oh! O Dick!" cried Lisbeth at this moment, "Dick—there's Aunt!"

"Aunt?" I repeated.

"Aunt Agatha, and she sees us; look!"

Turning my head, I beheld a most unexpected sight. Advancing directly upon us was the old boat, that identical, weather-beaten tub of a boat in which Lisbeth and I had come so near ending our lives together, the which has already been told in these Chronicles. On the rowing-thwart sat Peter, the coachman, and in the stern-sheets, very grim and stiff in the back, her lorgnettes at her eyes, was Lady Warburton.

Escape was quite out of the question, and in half a dozen strokes of the oar we were alongside and close under the battery of the lorgnettes.

"Elizabeth," she began in her most ponderous manner, ignoring my presence altogether, "Elizabeth, child, I blush for you."

"Then, Aunt, please don't," cried Lisbeth; "I can do quite enough of that for myself. I'm always blushing lately," and as if to prove her words she immediately proceeded to do so.

"Elizabeth," proceeded Lady Warburton, making great play with her lorgnettes, "your very shameless, ungrateful letter I received last night. This morning I arose at an objectionably early hour, travelled down in a draughty train, and here I am out on a damp and nasty river in a leaky boat, with my feet horribly wet, but determined to save you from an act which you may repent all your days."

"Excuse me," I said, bowing deeply, "but such heroic devotion cannot be sufficiently appreciated and admired. In Lisbeth's name I beg to thank you; nevertheless——"

"Mr. Brent, I believe?" she said in a tone of faint surprise, as though noticing my presence for the first time.

"At your service, madam!" I answered with another bow.

"Then I must ask you to convey my ward back to Fane Court immediately; she and the children will accompany me to London at once."

"My dear Lady Warburton," I said, fronting the lorgnettes with really admirable fortitude, "it grieves me to deny you this request, but believe me, it is impossible!"

"Impossible!" she repeated.

"Quite!" I answered. "You here behold the good ship *Joyful Hope,* bound for the 'Land of Heart's Delight,' and we aboard are all determined on our course."

" 'An' the wind blows fair, an' our helm's a-lee, so it's heave, my mariners, all—O!' " cried the Imp in his nautical voice.

"Dear me!" ejaculated Lady Warburton, staring. "Elizabeth, be so obliging as to tell me what it all means. Why have you dragged these children from their beds to come philandering upon a horrid river at such an hour?"

"Excuse me, Aunt, but she didn't drag us," protested the Imp, bowing exactly as I had done a moment before.

"Oh, no, we came," nodded Dorothy.

"An' we've been getting married, you know," said the Imp.

"And it was all very, very beautiful," added Dorothy; "even Louise enjoyed it ever so much!" and she kissed the fluffy kitten.

"Married!" cried Lady Warburton in a tone of horror; "married!"

"They would do it, you know," sighed the Imp.

"And quite right, too," said Dorothy; "everybody always marries somebody, some time; it's very fashionable at present. Mamma did and so shall I when I grow up, I suppose."

"Goodness gracious, child!" exclaimed Lady Warburton.

"I s'pose you're angry 'bout it, Aunt," pursued the Imp. "I was at first—just a weeny bit; but you see

MY LADY CAPRICE

Uncle Dick has a wonderful house
with swords an' armour, but empty,
an' he wanted to keep somebody in it
to see that everything was nice, I
s'pose, an' sing, you know, an' take
care of his life. Auntie Lisbeth can
sing, an' she wanted to go, so I forgave them."

"Oh, indeed, Reginald?" said Lady
Warburton in a rather queer voice,
and I saw the corners of her high,
thin nose quiver strangely.

"Beggin' your pardon, ma'am," said
Peter at this moment, touching his
cap, "I don't · know much about
boats, my line bein' 'osses, but I do
think as this 'ere boat is a-goin' to
sink."

"Then row for the shore instantly,"
said Lady Warburton firmly, "and
should I never reach it alive"—here
she brought her lorgnette to bear on
Lisbeth—"I say if I *do* meet a watery
grave this day, my epitaph shall be,

ᗖ 281 ᗕ

'Drowned by the Ingratitude of a Niece.' "

However, this gloomy tragedy being happily averted, and Lady Warburton safely landed, I, at a nod from Lisbeth, rowed to the bank likewise and we all disembarked together.

Now, as kind Fortune would have it, and Fortune was very kind that morning, the place where we stood was within a stone's throw of The Three Jolly Anglers, and wafted to us on the warm, still air there came a wondrous fragrance, far sweeter and more alluring than the breath of roses or honeysuckle—the delightful aroma of frying bacon.

Lady Warburton faced us, her parasol tucked beneath her arm, looking very much like a military officer on parade.

"Dorothy and Reginald," she said in a short, sharp voice of command, "bid good-bye to your Auntie Lisbeth and accompany me home at once."

"No, no," cried Lisbeth, with hands stretched out appealingly, "you will not leave us like this, Aunt—for the sake of the love I shall always bear you, and—and——"

"Elizabeth, I cared for you from your babyhood up. Ingratitude is my return. I watched you grow from child to woman. I planned out a future for you; you broke those plans. I might tell you that I am a lonely, disappointed old woman, who loved you much more than she thought, but I won't!"

"Dear, dear Aunt Agatha, did you love me so much, and I never guessed; you wouldn't let me, you see. Ah! do not think me ungrateful, but when a woman comes to marry she must choose for herself as I have done; and I am happy, dear, and proud of my choice—proud to have won the true

love of a true man; only do not think
I am ungrateful. And if this must be
good-bye, do not let us part like this—
for my sake and your sake and the
sake of my—husband."

Lady Warburton had turned away,
and there ensued a somewhat embar-
rassing pause.

"Elizabeth," she said suddenly, "if
I don't mistake, somebody is frying
bacon somewhere, and I'm ravenously
hungry."

"So am I," cried the Imp.

"And so am I," Dorothy chimed in.

"Then suppose we have breakfast,"
I suggested, and in almost less time
than it takes to tell I was leading the
way across the green with Lady Warburton on my arm—actually leaning
on my arm. It all happened so
quickly that Heaven and Lisbeth alone
know how she got there.

And now who so surprised to see us
as honest Amos Baggett, ushering us

with many bows and smiles into the Sanded Parlour, where breakfast was soon ready; and who so quick and dexterous in attending to our wants as the rosy-cheeked chambermaid?

And what a breakfast that was! Never had the antique andirons on the hearth, the pewter plates and dishes upon the walls, the brass-bound blunderbuss above the mantel seemed so bright and polished before, and surely never had they gleamed upon a merrier company. To be sure, the Imp's remarks were somewhat few and far between, but that was simply on account of the blackberry jam.

"I suppose you are both ridiculously happy," said Lady Warburton, eyeing us over her coffee cup.

"Most absurdly!" answered Lisbeth, blushing all in a moment.

"Preposterously!" I nodded.

"Of course!" said Lady Warburton, and setting down her cup, she sighed, while I wondered what memories her narrow life could hold.

"Uncle Dick," said the Imp suddenly, "do you s'pose Scarlet Sam ever ate blackberry jam?"

"Undoubtedly, my Imp, when he could get it." This appeared to greatly relieve his mind, for he took another helping.

But all things must have an end, alas!—even such a breakfast as this, and presently we were out in the sunshine again, standing beneath the weather-beaten sign whereon three faded fishermen fished with faded rods in a faded stream; while away down the road we could see Peter already approaching with the carriage.

"And now I suppose you are going?" said Lady Warburton.

"There is a train at half-past ten," I answered.

"An' we are going, too!" said Dorothy.

"Yes, we're quite ready, Uncle Dick," cried the Imp, thrusting his pistols into his belt.

"But you wouldn't leave me all alone, would you, children?" asked Lady Warburton, and there was a certain wistfulness in her sharp face that seemed new to it.

"'Course not," sighed the Imp, "only——

"We must stay and take care of her, Reginald," nodded Dorothy decisively.

"Yes, I'll take care of you, Aunt, with lance, battle-axe, an' sword, by day an' night," said the Imp, "only—I should have liked to see Uncle Dick's wonderful house, with the real swords an' armour, in the Land of Heart's Delight — some day, you know."

"And so you shall," cried Lady Warburton, and she actually stooped to kiss him, and then Dorothy, rather 'pecky' kisses, perhaps, but very genuine kisses notwithstanding.

"Richard," she said, giving me her hand, "we shall come down to your wonderful house—all three of us next week, so be prepared—now be off—both of you."

"Then you forgive me, Aunt?" asked Lisbeth, hesitating.

"Well, I don't quite know yet, Lisbeth; but, my dear, I'll tell you something I have never mentioned to a living soul but you; if I had acted forty years ago as you did to-day, I should have been a very different creature to the cross-grained old woman you think me. There—there's a kiss, but as for forgiving you—that is quite another matter; I must have time to think it all over. Good-bye, my dear; and, Richard, fill her life with happiness, to make up for mine, if you can. Children, bid good-bye to your Auntie —and Uncle Dick!"

"You won't forget the sword with the 'deadly point,' will you, Uncle Dick?"

"I won't forget, my Imp!" Hereupon he tried to smile, but his trembling lips refused, and snatching his hand from mine he turned away; as for Dorothy, she was sobbing into the fur of the fluffy kitten.

Then I helped Lisbeth aboard *The Jopful Hope,* loving her the more for the tears that gleamed beneath her long lashes, and 'casting loose,' we glided out into the stream.

There they stood, the two children, with the white-haired figure between them, Dorothy holding up the round-eyed "Louise" for a parting glimpse, and the Imp flourishing his cutlass, until a bend of the river hid them from view.

So Lisbeth and I sailed on together through the golden morning to "The Land of Heart's Delight."

Lightning Source UK Ltd.
Milton Keynes UK
UKOW042329280912

199827UK00001B/156/P